CAPTURED

Willow Danes

CAPTURED
by Willow Danes

©2014 Here be Dragons

Cover Design: Steven James Catizone

Published by Here Be Dragons

ISBN-13: 978-0692271810
ISBN-10: 0692271813

Also available in eBook publication

PRINTED IN THE UNITED STATES OF AMERICA

ONE

The screaming came from overhead, like metal ripping through the sky.

In the next instant Jenna stumbled, falling onto her hands and knees as the cabin itself seemed to be lifted up a bit before being slammed back down in a puff of dust, the books and boxes and Pap's many doohickeys rattling around her.

She was gasping, her ears still ringing as the cabin settled into quiet again. Shaking, Jenna eased back onto her haunches, her hand going to the little golden bird charm that hung on a chain around her neck.

Earthquake?

Quakes were rare in this part of North Carolina, and besides, she'd felt that tremble, that rumbling, beneath her feet a few times out west and this was *nothing* like that.

Jenna's glance darted about the room—the half-packed boxes, the groupings she'd made as she sorted her grandfather's things into piles of stuff to keep or give away or throw out. Through the cabin's front window, she caught sight of a far-off spray of snow thrown high into the air and now falling rapidly to the ground.

When she'd fallen, she'd dropped the framed photo of her and Pap standing in front of The Sweet Tooth on opening day. Thankfully it hadn't broken, but the faded oval rag rug had done little to protect her knees from the fall and her palms felt raw and scraped.

Shakily Jenna placed the picture on the coffee table, put a hand on the worn red and black plaid sofa, and, wincing, got to her feet. Her right knee was likely going to sport a nasty bruise tomorrow but the couple steps across the living room to the window assured her that would be the worst of it. She frowned out at the sunny, snow-covered landscape, her breath fogging up the windowpane.

Plane crash, maybe?

There was a tiny airport not far from here. Recently built and meant for small craft—a few of the new, wealthy residents of Brittle Bridge used it when they didn't want to go to Six Oaks—it was little more than a runway and a couple hangars.

Jenna scanned the woods, looking for smoke, but even the snow had settled now and the mountain seemed peaceful as ever. It took her a moment to realize that the TV that she'd had on to keep her company while she tended to the heartrending task of packing up Pap's things had gone dark. A quick look at the blinking red light showed the Wi-Fi was out too.

No satellite, no Internet.

"Great," she muttered, rubbing her forehead with her fingertips. Thinking she could get by fine with just her cell she'd made the mistake of having the landline cut off last week before she realized her fancy—and expensive—new phone didn't work inside the cabin. Outside, sure. Go twenty feet or sit in the SUV and the damned thing worked perfectly.

Jenna chewed the inside of her cheek. She hadn't seen anything except the now-resettled spray of snow but if it *were* a downed plane then someone could be hurt out there. It got dark around five this time of year so there were a few hours of daylight left at least and she knew these woods better than anyone—excepting her grandfather, of course.

She grabbed her cell off the coffee table and in a few moments had her white down jacket zipped, the hood yanked up, and her gloves on. She was already wearing her sheepskin boots; the cabin floor sometimes felt cold to her even in the summer and now in January it was bitterly so.

Jenna drew in the bracing smell of snow and pine as she stepped onto the porch and shut the front door behind her. She was careful going down the cabin's front steps; she'd slipped often enough on them over the years to remember to hold the handrail in winter. The soft powdery snow crunched under her boots as she walked and, as expected, three steps past her SUV the cell had reception again.

She scrolled through the numbers to the right one and hit "Dial" as she headed in the direction where she'd seen the snow spray.

"Sheriff's Department."

"Sarah Jane? It's Jenna McNally."

"Hey there, Jenna, you okay?" Sarah Jane had once been a model, or so Pap had said. Got her heart broke by a famous artist in New York and fled to Brittle Bridge to escape it all.

But then again, he'd made up stories about everyone with Jenna—the mayor was in the witness protection program, her teacher was a secret agent. She'd been labeled a "sensitive child" by the social worker who had handled the transfer of custody to him. Of course to Pap "sensitive" meant "creative" so he'd gone all out in encouraging her in all of it—the arts and music, crafting, baking—anything she wanted to try, and he was proud as punch to let her.

But if Sarah Jane had been a model, it was thirty-five years ago or more now and twenty since she joined the sheriff's department. "You up at Pap's still?"

Her grandfather's name was William James McNally. But it had probably been since before Sarah Jane's supposed model-artist affair days that he had been called anything other than "Pap" in the vicinity of Brittle Bridge—at least never in the twenty-six years Jenna had known him.

Well, excepting that social worker.

"Yeah, I'll be here for a couple more days," Jenna said, already past the clearing around the house and into the forest. "Listen, I think a plane crashed up here on our"—she swallowed hard—"my land."

"A plane?" Sarah Jane's voice went from neighborly to official. "Where did it come down?"

"Not sure." Jenna ducked under a branch as she headed deeper into the woods. "I heard something real loud and then it was like 'bam,' something hitting the ground hard. Shook the whole place."

"Can you see smoke from where you are now?"

"No," Jenna admitted, trotting along as fast as the snow would allow her. Some of the drifts were deep and she had to mind where she stepped. She wouldn't be doing anyone any good if she broke her ankle. "I'm heading out to take a look now."

"But you *saw* the plane go down?"

"Uh, no." Sarah Jane's too-patient tone was starting to make her feel a little embarrassed for calling when she hadn't actually seen anything. Maybe it *was* something else: a really big tree falling or a damn meteorite or something.

"Huh," Sarah Jane said. "Lemme call around and see if anybody's gone missing. But you call me straight off if you find anything, 'kay?"

"Sure thing." Jenna ended the call and slipped the phone into her jacket pocket. Whatever crashed couldn't be far from where she'd seen the snow spray up.

Forced by the lack of schools and friends for his young granddaughter, Pap had kept the house in Asheville, but they'd come to Brittle Bridge at every opportunity. Pap's heart was here and she'd happily spent the summer days running barefooted in these woods clad in overalls, her chestnut hair in pigtails at first, then tied back in a ponytail as she got older.

Her stride faltered and she steadied herself against a pine, the rough trunk pulling on her knitted glove. Pap's beloved woods were quiet and bright around her but Jenna suddenly had a strong urge to run back to the cabin.

She set her jaw and pressed on. Pap hadn't raised her to be a coward and this was *her* land now. He'd left her five hundred acres and anyone on it without her say-so was trespassing, even if it was about to go up for sale.

Still, she wished she'd thought to grab Pap's revolver or rifle or even his hunting knife before she'd come racing down here.

I'll go as far as the creek and if I don't find anything I'll head on back.

But all was quiet at the creek too, the crystal clear water moving placidly between the banks—

Jenna stopped short. There was tang to the air, a burned smell that wrinkled her nose. It reminded her a little bit of the inside of a mechanic's garage, out of place in such pristine woods.

It smelled *wrong*. Not only that…

There's no snow here.

There was snow all around, covering the ground, hanging heavy in the tree limbs above, but *here* there was just a long patch of mud and broken sticks.

The sudden sick feeling of being watched raised the tiny hairs on the back of her neck. With a shock of awareness she realized just how very vulnerable she was out here, alone and unarmed.

Pap hadn't raised her to be an idiot either. With trembling fingers she pulled her phone out and hit redial to the Sheriff's office.

In horrified disbelief she watched the screen flash *"Connection failed."*

She took a step back and searched the silent, still forest.

All I have to do is make it back up to the house. I can get the gun, get my car keys, call for help, get the hell out of here!

Her quickened breath was visible as she headed uphill back toward the cabin, the drifts and her fear slowing her down. She couldn't remember if the ammunition was still in the kitchen cabinet or if she'd moved it to—

Something off to her right gave a soft, deep growl.

Jenna skidded to a halt, scanning the woods again, but the growling had already stopped. She pulled off her hood to see—and hear—better, yanking a bit of her long hair painfully in the process.

Black bears didn't growl; that only happened in the movies. They would huff sometimes or moan but they absolutely *didn't* growl.

Oh, God, it's a fucking wolf!

Jenna wet her lips. There was a broken tree limb near her right foot and she fumbled for it, dropping her cell in her hurry, her gloved fingers digging in the snow to get hold of the branch.

She brought the limb up, wielding it like a baseball bat. Her glance darted about, her rough weapon gripped tightly in her hands.

A startled scream tore from her throat at the rush of movement.

Two deer burst from the tree line, their hooves kicking up snow and dirt as they bounded away. Jenna stood still, her heart hammering even as the hoof beats of the retreating deer grew fainter.

Then the forest was peaceful again, the sun sparkling on the snow.

Standing in the woods where she'd spent every summer, school break, and holiday, she started to wonder if she'd imagined that growl in the first place.

The strain of losing Pap, then the funeral and having to come back here where he had warmly made room for her in his life, was more than enough already. And now, readying the place for sale had worn her nerves raw. Remembering how it had often been just the two of them fishing and reading and talking, having to pack all those wonderful sunlit days up into cardboard boxes and know they were gone forever left her feeling like she was standing at the top of a staircase and the stairs behind her had just vanished.

Jenna took a deep breath and let it out slowly, lowering the branch. She'd gotten spooked was all. Best just head back to the cabin, check in with Sarah Jane, and get to packing.

Her pricy phone was still lying in the snow where she'd dropped it. She sighed. Praying it had survived the fall and the snow, Jenna shifted the branch to her left hand and bent down to get it.

A shadow rose up in front of her.

He—definitely male—was huge. Easily seven feet tall, broad as a linebacker, he had long, shaggy blue-black hair that skimmed his shoulders and hung down his back. His skin was tanned in tone, and his clothing looked like dark brown leather wrapped around him, but it was neither his size nor his odd attire that kept her frozen in place—it was his face.

His forehead was rippled—that was the only word for it—and his brow ridges heavy. The cheekbones of his square-jawed face were high, his mouth full. It was a masculine face, a fierce, terrifying one.

And it *wasn't* human.

His eyes were unlike any eyes should be. From beneath black eyebrows they glowed an electric blue color, fixed on her like a predator's.

His full lips drew back to reveal the sharp, long canines of a beast and his roar shattered the peaceful woods.

Screaming, Jenna fell backward into the snow, the branch torn from her hand. He pulled a weapon from the holster at his hip and she scrambled back as he came toward her, snarling.

She threw her hand up to protect her face as he leveled the weapon at her and fired—

Two

Jenna groaned.

She forced her eyes open a little, wincing against the throbbing in her head as the beamed ceiling of her bedroom came into focus. She recognized the familiar feel of her mattress beneath her, the softness of her old patchwork quilt under her palm, the feather pillow cradling her head.

Jenna swallowed against the painful, raw dryness in her mouth. The door to her room was open a crack. The fire she'd lit earlier was still burning but it was dark outside now.

She'd felt woozy like this once before, when she'd gotten real sick with the flu. So ill that Pap had to take her to the hospital for IV fluids, his chocolate brown eyes, so like her own, reflecting his worry even as he made up stories about the doctors and nurses being spies, deep under cover, to distract both of them.

Jenna tried to sit up now and couldn't.

Her right wrist was cuffed to the bedpost.

Startled to full wakefulness, she blinked in astonishment at the restraint holding her. They might be doing the job of handcuffs but they sure didn't look like any she'd ever seen. By the faint light coming in through the partly opened bedroom door, the cuffs were a light gray metal. The cuff around her wrist was wide as four of her fingers and fit her wrist with perfect smoothness. At the end of a thick cord the other handcuff—if it could be called that—was thicker, narrow, and wrapped solidly around the wooden bedpost.

The image of that creature out in the woods flashed through her mind.

He shot me!

Her hand went to her chest, her ribs, but there was no wound and she didn't feel any pain.

Some kind of stun gun?

She was alone in the bedroom but it took her only a moment to put together it was probably *he* who had cuffed her. That meant he might still be nearby. He could be in the house right now and she was manacled to the bed!

Oh, God! Oh, God!

She was still clad in her jeans and sweater but her boots and socks were off, her white jacket thrown across the chair near the bedroom door. Her glance darted around the room only to find everything else looked as she had left it this morning.

The clock on the bedside table read 8:37. That meant she'd been knocked out for almost six hours.

She strained to hear but couldn't detect anything other than her own shallow breathing and the crackling of the fire in the living room.

I have to get out of here!

Heart hammering, she tugged hard, wincing at the noise the cord made as it scraped against the wood. She rolled onto her right side and felt around the cuff with her left hand for a catch but the thing felt as smooth as if it had been formed around her wrist.

Heavy footsteps crossed the living room, heading her way and sending her heart racing even faster. Jenna pulled against the bedpost, shaking the bed to a rattle in her desperation.

The door swung open. Jenna gave a cry, cowering against the headboard as a huge form filled the doorway.

She trembled there, drawing quick, frightened breaths, but he didn't move toward her. Backlit by the fire as he was, she couldn't make out anything but a shadowy outline. Still, from the size of him there was no question it was the same beast she'd seen in the forest.

Not being able to see anything but that huge black shadow was unbearable. After a few moments, Jenna reached a shaking hand toward the bedside table and yanked the lamp's thin metal chain.

He startled when the light cut on. His wild black hair shook a bit with his flinch and he gave a fang-flashing snarl at the sudden illumination in the room.

God, it was better with the light off...

His eyes had round black pupils like a human's but the irises glowed in an absolutely eerie inhuman way as they fixed on her. He was also every bit as huge and broad-shouldered as she remembered. Through his close-cut dark brown clothing she could see the shape of his powerful muscles. His hands looked like they could crush rocks.

The existence-bending fact that there was a living, breathing, intelligent being *that wasn't human* standing in her bedroom was blotted out by her realization he also was still armed. The gun belt was worn at his hip and strapped onto his muscular thigh. The weapon he'd used on her earlier was holstered there too.

But he didn't move toward her or reach for his gun. Her body was curled in a tight, uncomfortable pose and after a few heartbeats she risked shifting her position a bit.

"What—what do you want?" she got out.

He tilted his head.

"What do you want?" Jenna demanded, louder this time.

He took a step toward her and she whimpered, cringing against the bed pillows and headboard.

He stopped short. His lips drew back, his fangs wickedly sharp in the light, and he gave a soft, low growl.

"Please . . ." Jenna wet her lips. "Please don't hurt me."

He pivoted, gone from the room so swiftly that she was left blinking. For someone that huge he moved really goddamned *fast*.

The restraint around her wrist was some kind of metal, weirdly warm to the touch and smooth. Interesting and all— she would be thrilled to ponder it further once she got the hell out of here. Her frenzied pulls and fumbling searches for the catch weren't getting her anywhere.

So I'll break the fucking bedpost!

She wasn't sure how long he would be gone and he knew she was conscious so subtlety be damned. She got on her knees and threw her weight against the headboard, knocking it into the wall, but it was good North Carolina pine and the bedpost too thick to crack. She tried to slide the restraint upwards around the bedpost instead. There was a decorative knob there; carved, not screwed on, but maybe she could—

One moment he wasn't there in the doorway, the next he was. Jenna gave a short startled cry at his sudden reappearance and froze, still straining to get the manacle past the bedpost knob.

His unnerving glance took in her position against the headboard then he met her eyes again. He held her gaze as he approached; his movements were as smooth as a stalking panther, startling in someone his size.

He'd looked big before; this close he made her five-foot, eight-inch frame seem positively delicate. The bed dipped under his weight as he knelt on the quilt, facing her, but even in this position he loomed over her. She caught the scent of him then, warm, male, almost cinnamon-like.

Jenna flinched as his hand came up toward her face and he froze. After a few heartbeats where he stayed disconcertingly still, he reached for her again, slower this time. Jenna could feel her lips trembling as he stroked her hair.

His fingers felt calloused as he touched her temple, tracing along her skin, skimming the curve of her cheek to her jaw. He tilted her chin up, the pad of his thumb running over her chinbone as he studied her face.

His electric blue gaze met hers.

Then, very softly, so softly it seemed half purr, he growled.

The sound vibrated through her body and sent a startling, tingling rush of warmth through her belly to tighten her center. On the heels of that wave her breasts felt heavy, her nipples nearly as sensitive as her clit suddenly felt.

Heat flashed in his vivid eyes and her face warmed at the realization that he knew exactly what her reaction to his rumble had been. She wet her lips and his eyes were drawn immediately there, his gaze now fixed on her mouth.

It had been a long time since she'd been with anyone. Tending her grandfather during his illness, running the bakery, then moving up here to see to it Pap left this life in the comfort and dignity of his own home had been way more important than getting, or keeping, a boyfriend. Two years without so much as a kiss had to be why she'd even be *thinking*—

Jenna cleared her throat and the alien seemed startled by the sound. She tore her gaze away from those gleaming blue eyes for an instant to send a pointed look at her manacled wrist.

"Please let me go."

His gaze was unnervingly intent on hers.

"Just let me go, okay?" she whispered, pulling against the restraint.

He had a strap across his chest and as he lifted it she realized he had gone to get a pack of the same dark brown leather as his clothing. He put the bag on the bed and she turned her body toward him as he shifted to sit beside her.

He opened the satchel and rifled around before pulling out a soft pouch about the size of his hand. He fiddled with it then detached a straw-like tube and brought it to her mouth.

She reared back. "What's that?"

He looked puzzled and examined the tube. Apparently concluding that *it* wasn't the problem he tried to push the thing at her mouth again.

She twisted her head away and he made a huffing, frustrated noise.

With slow, deliberate movements he put the tube into his own mouth and drew on it. He held her gaze as if trying to make sure she understood then took the straw from his mouth and put it to hers.

"No thanks," she stammered, trying to evade the tube. "Look, I don't want a drink. I want you to get this damned thing off me." For emphasis she yanked against the restraint.

He glanced at her wrist. He growled and jerked his chin at her.

Then he held the straw to her mouth again, his eyes bright, leaning forward as if to urge her on.

Jenna nipped the inside of her lip. Whatever was in that bag might be just dandy for aliens and real bad news for humans. But maybe if she played along she could get the restraints off and make it to Pap's rifle or out the front door.

"Okay, I guess we'll try it your way," she muttered and let him put the tube in her mouth.

Expecting some kind of disgusting alien sludge she was surprised to find it was simply water. She was parched but didn't want to drink too much of it, just in case it had some weird alien microbes in it or something. But just the little bit she took seemed to satisfy him.

He put the water bag back into his pack and took out a different container. When he unsealed it, she caught the scent of unfamiliar spices and meat. He broke off a piece between his thumb and forefinger then held it out to her.

"Uh, no, thanks."

He growled and touched it to her lips.

Jenna glanced nervously at whatever it was he held to her mouth but she didn't see that she had much in the way of options here.

"Fine," she said. "Making friends, right?"

She opened her mouth so he could feed her the morsel.

"Mmmm," she said, exaggerating the *yum* sound for him as she chewed, and he really did look pleased about that. Actually it wasn't bad; it tasted a bit like beef jerky. "Delicious, really. Now, maybe you could take the handcuff off me?"

He leaned toward her, his huge hand pressing into the mattress beside her, and with shocked awareness Jenna realized he was going to kiss her. She felt the heat radiating off his body, and breathed in the warmth of his masculine, cinnamon scent as he bent his head toward hers.

But he didn't kiss her.

Instead he gently rubbed his nose up one side of hers, tilted his face then rubbed down the other side, all the while making that soft, rumbly purr that sent heat curling through her belly.

He drew back to look at her, his blue eyes darkened with desire. She tried to reach for him and found her wrist still restrained.

She blinked, struggling to think against the insistent throbbing at her center.

Right. Escape from the alien.

"Maybe," she began faintly, "you could take the cuff off now?"

He leaned forward, rumbling again, and this time he nuzzled her neck.

"Oh, God," she breathed, letting her head fall back as his mouth brushed over her skin and that rumbling went right through her to vibrate her clit.

He was either *very* clean-shaven or didn't grow hair on his face because he didn't have any stubble at all. The softness of his hair brushed her cheek and jaw as he bent against her and before she knew it her free hand was on his shoulder, urging him closer. The muscle under her palm was rock solid, his body fever hot as if his body temperature were naturally much higher than hers.

His large hand went to the curve of her waist to pull her against him. He brushed her nose lightly up one side and down the other then, his eyes half-closed, lowered his head to nuzzle, his nose pressed to her skin as he breathed in and a fine tremble ran through his body. His hand came up to her breast and the feel of those long fingers brushing her nipple made her breath catch.

The reaction drew his attention and he pulled away to focus his fevered gaze there, the rumble coming from deeper in his broad chest. He cupped her breast, rubbing his thumb over her peak, watching her response. Jenna's mouth parted in a groan at the sensation and when he bent to nuzzle her again she tried to catch his mouth in a kiss.

He jerked back and his rumbling stopped instantly.

His shocked stare at her parted lips made her face go hot and she shut her mouth so quickly her teeth clicked.

His ridged brow creased and he moved further away to regard her with puzzled, alien eyes.

Jenna trembled, shaken by how fast and powerfully he'd roused her. If he hadn't stopped when he did she would have been pulling him down on top of her.

He studied her for a moment and then reached back into the bag and took out the meat stuff again. He broke off another piece and offered it to her.

Jenna turned her face away. "Uh, no, thanks. I'm good."

He pushed it at her and growled.

"No, really," she said, trying to evade the morsel that he held to her mouth. "I don't want any more."

He gave a frustrated snarl, trying feed her.

"Goddamn it! I'm not hungry!"

"*Grrrreeee*," he growled.

She blinked. *Did he just talk?*

His gaze held hers, his luminescent blue eyes intent as if he were waiting for something.

Or waiting for her to *do* something.

Jenna wet her lips. "Hungry."

He watched her mouth as she formed the word then growled, "*Huunnngggreeee.*"

"Right. *Not* hungry."

"*Gnootteeehuunngreee.*"

She searched his face then glanced at the cuff around her wrist. She held his gaze and pulled on it. "Let me go."

His brow furrowed, his eyes searching her face.

"Let me go, okay?"

He tilted his head. "*Gooookaaayyy?*"

She nodded and pulled on the cuff again. "Let me go. Please?"

With a glance at the restraint, he resealed the package and tucked it back into the pack. He leaned in close, his hand reaching around her, and in the next instant the cuff released. Jenna immediately pulled free to rub her wrist with her other hand. Her wrist didn't hurt but the air against her flesh felt odd, as if her skin had been wrapped in a bandage too long or something.

As he slipped the cuffs into his pack he caught sight of her rubbing at her skin and frowned. He took her hand in both of his, examining her wrist. Just his light touch as he turned her hand this way and that, his thumbs probing the bones and tendons of her wrist, had her breath quickening.

Jenna eased her hand out of his grip and scooted back. He didn't grab at her or roar or anything so after a moment she risked moving further across the bed.

As soon as she got to the other side she stood, fingering her bird charm necklace, the wood floor freezing cold under her bare feet. The alien watched but he didn't look angry or threatening and those wicked fangs of his didn't make an appearance either.

She didn't see her socks but spied her sheepskin boots near the closet door. She kept her eyes on the alien and eased over that way. Balancing on one foot then the other, she pulled her boots on.

That action got him to his feet; his body angled toward her but he didn't block the door or rush her. He just stood there, watching her with his brilliant eyes.

Jenna drew a slow, steadying breath. *Okay, now that we're all friendly like, let's see how far I can take this. Maybe I can just walk right the hell out of here.*

Her mouth dry and anticipating an attack any second, Jenna glanced toward the bedroom door and took a shaky step forward.

The alien's fangs flashed and he whirled that way, quivering tension clear in every muscle of his body. His arm came up and it was so clear a signal for her to hold position that, startled, she stopped where she was. He crept forward with his catlike movements to the doorway, looking this way and that. He sniffed at the air, his hand on the weapon at his hip.

After a few moments his stance eased and he looked back at her quizzically.

It took her a second to figure it out.

He thinks there's something in the cabin scaring me.

She swallowed hard. *Does he really not know it's him?*

She grabbed her jacket off the bedroom chair as she went by and pulled it on. With slow—hopefully nonthreatening—movements she went past him into the living room and he followed her. Between the light from the bedroom and the fire she could see fine. But she knew this place so well she could have moved around in pitch-blackness.

What she *couldn't* do was remember where she'd left her fucking car keys.

She patted the pockets of her jacket just to be sure but of course they weren't there. The alien eyed her but he didn't seem to consider what she was doing a threat. Her phone was still out in the woods somewhere, but between the dark and the snow she was never going to find it tonight to call for help. Even if she managed to get past him and outdoors, he moved like quicksilver. She'd never outrun him.

And that meant her only chance was to make it to the SUV.

Her bag was on the coffee table. He seemed fascinated by her every move as she headed to the table and picked up her purse. She kept her eyes on him as she dug her hand through her bag but he simply watched as she rifled around. She was getting ready to dump the contents out on the table when a flash of metal caught her eye.

Her car keys were right there.

On his gun belt.

Swallowing hard, she put her bag down and took a step toward him.

"Hey." She forced a smile and gestured at his belt. "Think maybe I could get my keys back?"

He blinked. Then in a flash of almost-human squared off white teeth and *definitely*-not-human fangs he smiled back.

His grin was charming, sexy, and utterly terrifying.

Caught between the endearment of it and stomach-twisting fear, Jenna's smile froze.

His grin faded and he gave a soft, inquisitive growl.

She tried to focus on taking those slow, even breaths she'd learned in yoga class as she moved closer.

It wasn't helping much.

"My keys?" she asked, her voice high-pitched with fear, near enough now she felt the warmth radiating off his body. She stretched her hand out, slowly reaching for his gun belt. "I'm just going to take my keys back, okay?"

You stunned me or something and you cuffed me but maybe you weren't trying to hurt me. Maybe you won't now.

She hooked her finger through the key ring and raised her eyes to meet his glowing gaze.

I really, really hope you won't—

With a sudden flash of fangs, the alien gave an ear-splitting roar.

THREE

Jenna jumped back with a petrified squeak.

"Okay," she managed after a few moments when he didn't tear her head off, her whole body quaking. "Okay, not so much into giving back the keys right now."

The alien's black brows came together but he looked more surprised and puzzled than angry. He leaned down, searching her eyes, then he made a soft, soothing growl that almost made her forget she was terrified of him.

She swallowed hard. *Well, now what the hell do I do?*

Heavy flakes pattered against the windowpanes. It was a January night in the Smoky Mountains and her cell was somewhere out there in the snow. Even if she managed to elude a creature who moved like lightning, even if she made it outdoors, she would be trading a warm, stocked cabin with an alien who didn't seem inclined to hurt her—as long as she didn't touch her keys apparently—for the virtual guarantee of getting lost in the dark and freezing to death outside.

And that left her with two choices: get the car keys sometime tonight or wait for daylight to make a run for it.

Either way, I'm not going anywhere any time soon.

"All righty, then," she muttered, pushing her hair behind her ears. "Don't know about you but I missed supper."

She also really, *really* needed to pee.

Pulling off the down jacket, she headed for the coat tree by the front door. He followed, probably intending to block her escape if she'd had a mind for it as she hung her coat on one of the hooks.

She flipped the living room lights' switch and his startled glance took in the space, then came back to rest on her.

"I'm going to the bathroom," she said, heading in that direction.

He was immediately at her heels. She turned in the bathroom doorway and held her hand up to stop him.

"I'll be right out," she promised, still holding her hand up to him in the "stay" position, but he caught the door with the palm of his hand before she could close it. She pushed a little harder. Then harder still, digging her heels into the bathroom's wood floor.

It was like trying to move a boulder with a toothpick.

"Oh, for fuck's sake!" she cried. "Will you let me pee already?"

Startled by her outburst, he let go and she slammed the door in his face then threw the lock. She had her jeans down and her butt on the seat in an instant. She rubbed her forehead against the headache coming on and closed her eyes in relief as she let her stream go.

The bathroom door burst open with enough force to bounce back off the wall behind it and Jenna let out a startled scream, her knees clutching together, bending over herself protectively.

The door's busted lock swung back and forth against the doorjamb as he took in her position with sharp, alien eyes.

Then he sniffed.

Understanding lit his face and he gave what sounded suspiciously like a growled chuckle. Still knock-kneed and bent over to cover herself, Jenna narrowed her gaze at him.

"Do you mind?" she gritted out.

He didn't appear to mind at all and ducking his head through the doorway walked right into the wood-paneled bathroom, examining the space with interest.

"Damn it, get *out!*" Jenna gave as stern a point as she could while sitting on the toilet with her jeans and panties around her calves. "I'm not kidding! *Out!*"

For certain he understood she wanted him gone. He just wasn't interested in going.

Jenna glared but clearly it was pee with him here or nothing.

"I don't believe this," she mumbled and, dropping her burning face in her hand, chose the former.

She was too embarrassed to meet his eye as she grabbed a handful of toilet paper. She yanked her panties and jeans up quick, not missing how he tilted his head, trying to get a look at her.

She flushed the toilet and, angry enough now not to be afraid, shoved past him to the sink. He watched that too, standing right behind her to look over her shoulder as she turned the handles, cutting on the water to wash her hands.

Unexpectedly his arms went around her, his big body warm against her back. He put his hands under the faucet with hers, spreading his fingers in the water.

Jenna hesitated, clutching the bar of honeysuckle soap. She glanced at him in the reflection as he took the soap from her, surprise showing on his face at the slipperiness of it. He rubbed it between his hands as she'd done, inhaling the scent, looking delighted at the resulting bubbles.

He met her gaze briefly in the mirror then put the soap down and caught her hands between his large, warm ones. Taking his time, his expression intent as if it were the most serious of things, he gently washed one of her hands then the other. He rinsed her hands with that same absorbed focus, the careful handling and utter tenderness of it making her throat tighten.

In her whole life no man had ever touched her like this—as if she were the most precious thing in the world and he was overwhelmed at simply being allowed to.

"Thank you," she murmured thickly, surprised to find she had to blink tears away.

She grabbed the towel hung next to the sink and dried her hands. Her cheeks warmed under that vivid alien gaze as she dried both of his too.

He was standing very close, searching her face, looking as if he were trying to memorize every curve and line.

Jenna ventured a shy smile and with a glimmer of fangs he smiled back, not as broadly this time, like he was afraid of frightening her with his grin as he had before.

God, he smells amazing.

"Okay," she muttered, twisting around to hang the towel up. "Maybe need to refocus here."

When she turned back he was still regarding her with the same intent interest. It was so tempting to grab that big hand of his, pull him back into her bedroom, and find out just what she needed to do to get him rumbling again . . .

"I'm hungry," she blurted. "What about you? You hungry?"

He didn't answer, of course, and he didn't move either. She had to shimmy past him to leave and he felt like solid warm muscle against her. He followed her into the kitchen, ducking his head through the doorway, his footsteps heavy on the wooden floor in those boots of his. She hadn't even started packing in here, intending to do it last. The fridge and cabinets were still full.

She opened the fridge, leaning against the side of the door as she scanned the contents.

What do you serve a seven-foot-tall alien for dinner?

"Whatever the hell he wants," she said under her breath.

Well, he'd fed her meat earlier so obviously he ate that.

"How about breakfast for dinner?" she asked, not expecting an answer, and grabbed a package of bacon and the carton of eggs from the fridge. "I make a great cheese omelet."

Jenna pulled the rest of the ingredients and started the cast iron pan heating for the bacon. She'd cook that first, then do the omelets in the bacon grease, country-style. She got the bread loaded into the toaster so she could drop them when the omelets were almost done.

As soon as she started the bacon frying the alien's sniffer went crazy.

He stood right beside her, his electric blue eyes dancing between her and the sizzling bacon with such hopeful eagerness that Jenna couldn't help but smile.

"Don't worry," she assured as she turned the strips. "I'm making plenty for both of us."

When the bacon was crisp she put the slices on paper towels to absorb the extra grease. As soon as it was cool enough to handle she gave him a slice.

He crushed the strip into his mouth in one bite, already reaching for the next. With four bites he finished off all the bacon she'd cooked.

"Wow," she managed. "I guess it's a good thing I have another whole package."

Of the next twelve slices of bacon she fried up she managed to snag only one but the look on his face was such pure bliss it was hard to complain.

"I guess they don't have cholesterol on your planet," she said, watching him lick the bacon grease from his fingers, rumbling in satisfaction.

At his size, he dwarfed the kitchen's battered old table and chairs and the fork looked almost comically small in his hand. He had some trouble copying how she cut her food with the edge of the fork so she grabbed a knife and cut his omelet into more manageable, bite-sized pieces for him. He wolfed down everything she'd given him with appreciative rumbles and she wound up giving him a third of her food to polish off as well.

Toast with butter and strawberry jam slathered on top brought him to a whole new level of happiness. Orange juice became a quick favorite too and he decimated half the Tropicana jug, pouring glass after glass for himself.

When he'd finished everything he sat back, looking at her with warm eyes.

"You know what?" Jenna gave him a quick smile. "I have an idea."

Her grandfather hadn't had much appetite in his last days and she hadn't had the heart for baking since, but she could still make Pap's favorite double-fudge chocolate chip brownies in her sleep. She pulled the ingredients and had the *mise en place* put together in minutes. The alien watched as she cracked eggs and measured cocoa and sugar. He stood at her side as she mixed, watching as she smoothed the batter into the pan.

She slid the pan into the oven and he stuck his hand inside before she could shut the door.

"Oh, careful," she cried, grabbing his wrist to pull his hand out. "You'll hurt yourself."

He watched her mouth as she spoke like he was trying to catch her words and gave a soft huff when she stopped.

The alien busied himself exploring the kitchen as she washed up. He opened and closed drawers, touching everything he could get his hands on, holding this or that up to the light to get a better look.

Glancing at him as she worked, she wondered if his vision was different than hers. Certainly he seemed to have a much better sense of smell; his eyes were alight with interest and he was sniffing at the oven long before she could smell the brownies at all. The timer went off just as she was finished wiping up the counter and he caught her wrist as she opened the oven door to take the pan out.

"It's okay," she assured, showing him she was going to use an oven mitt to protect her hand.

He hesitated then relaxed his grip, trailing his fingers along her palm as she pulled her hand away.

He inhaled deeply as she took the brownies out.

"We have to let them cool," she warned, waving him back. Jenna wasn't sure why she kept talking. It wasn't like he could understand her. It just made her feel more comfortable around him.

I shouldn't be comfortable. I shouldn't be enjoying this. He shot me! He handcuffed me to the bed. He's a fucking alien, for God's sake!

But she *was* enjoying this. Enjoying watching his face light up with each new taste, seeing his intent interest in every little thing she did, touching and examining things with the openhearted curiosity of a child.

"I gotta throw another log on the fire," she muttered, pushing past him into the living room.

She moved the fire gate aside, aware of how he tensed as she put the log on. She moved the gate back and straightened to find herself looking at one of the photos of her and Pap on the mantle.

It had been taken the summer before he'd gotten sick. Pap was smiling big, his rounded cheeks ruddy with good health. He was wearing his favorite battered fishing hat and vest, holding a catch the size of a goldfish. She was next to him, a couple inches taller than he, her cheeks and nose pink from the sun, a spray of freckles across her nose, her brown hair showing bits of gold, grinning too as she held up a ten-pound bass.

A lump formed in her throat. She reached for the bird charm she wore, the one he'd given her when she'd first come to live with him, her tears blurring his smiling face.

I miss you so much . . .

She startled when the alien touched her, his hand light as he cradled the back of her head, stroking her hair. She met his eyes and he blinked, his gaze following the progress of the tears on her face. He gently brushed away a tear from her face and rubbed the wetness between his fingers.

"That's my Pap," she said with a nod at the photo. "He . . . he died a little while ago. That's why I'm sad."

He glanced at the photo and back at her, his head tilted. She took the frame down and pointed at her grandfather. "Pap."

"Pppaaapp," he growled.

She gave a short laugh and wiped her nose with the back of her hand. "Hey, that was pretty good."

He pointed to the image of her.

"Well, that's me. I mean, obviously."

He waited, searching her face. He tapped the image of her again, more insistently this time.

She passed her hand over her eyes. "Right. Sorry. I'm an idiot. You want my name. *Jenna.*"

He jerked his chin sharply at her.

"My name is Jenna," she said, then more slowly and pointing to herself, "Jenna."

"Jjjeennnnaaa," he rumbled. He leaned closer, his callused hand cupping her face. "Jjjeeennnaaaa."

She caught herself rubbing her cheek against the warmth of his rough palm.

She cleared her throat. "What's your name? I mean, aliens must have names too, right?"

He was looking at her mouth again as if trying to decipher the stream of words.

She pointed at the photo. "Pap." She pointed at herself. "Jenna." Then she touched his chest, raising her eyebrows.

"Rrraaa'kkuurrr."

"Ra'kur?" she repeated, trying to mimic his rolling growl.

A smile flittered across his face but whether he was amused by her pronunciation or happy that she'd even come close she couldn't tell.

"Jjjeeennnaaaa. Rrraaa'kkuurrr." He took her hand and placed her palm against his chest, his hand over hers. She could feel his heart thumping under her palm. He growled something but whether it was a bunch of words or one really long one she couldn't even *begin* to say.

He seemed to be expecting something back so she offered a quick smile. "Jenna. Ra'kur."

She eased her hand out from under his and placed the photo back on the mantle. She took a shaky breath; Pap grinned back at her.

"Come on, Ra'kur." Jenna gave the alien a watery smile. "Let's get you a brownie."

FOUR

Maybe I should have gone with Parcheesi instead . . .

She got two tiny brownies and Ra'kur got the rest of the pan. By the time he'd polished off his stack of brownies, rumbling happily again, it wasn't even ten o'clock. He wasn't showing any signs of sleepiness for her to even think about snagging the car keys and this time of year the sun wouldn't rise till half past seven.

Jenna wasn't sure when he was going to fall asleep. Maybe he only slept once a week or something.

For all she knew, he never slept at all.

Being stuck without satellite left her with a bunch of musty-smelling board games and whatever old films were around to entertain her alien guest. Jenna unpacked some DVDs from the "donate" box trying to find something they could watch. Ra'kur examined the disks, turning them this way and that in the light, seeming just as fascinated by the mirror-like side as the printed one.

She flipped past *Rocky* and—oh-no-fucking-way— *Predator* and settled on *The Gentleman Rogue*.

Ra'kur sat beside her on the big plaid sofa—she had to move the coffee table to make room for his long legs— watching the costume romantic comedy with polite attention. Not being able to understand the Gentleman Rogue, Charles, and Lady Nell's snappy, flirty dialogue while the pair ran around Restoration England would no doubt make this film really boring but Jenna wanted him calm, maybe even sleepy, which was why she'd picked it.

Well, that and she'd forgotten all about the scene when the Rogue and Lady Nell kiss.

As soon as Charles laid one on Nell, Ra'kur sat bolt upright, his attention riveted to the screen. He leaned forward, studying as Charles and Nell fell back on the bed to get hot and heavy, their lacy, anachronistic undies flying.

When the scene cut to the next morning with the still-naked Rogue jumping out the window to escape the Duke and his men, Ra'kur turned wide, glowing eyes on her.

Jenna cringed, remembering how she'd tried to kiss him earlier.

"Yeah, listen, I . . . Hey!" she exclaimed, pushing herself up from the sofa. "How'd you like to try popcorn?"

She headed toward the kitchen but quicker than she could have believed possible Ra'kur was in front of her, blocking her way.

He reached out, lightly touching her mouth with two fingers, then he touched his own mouth, his eyes questioning.

"Yeah, sorry about that earlier," she said, ducking her head.

He repeated the action, touching her mouth, then his own.

"Nnnnammme," he growled.

"Oh, yeah. Right." Of course he just wanted the name for it. His earlier shocked reaction showed he wasn't interested in *doing* it. There were even some human cultures that found mouth kissing to be disgusting.

"It's called a kiss." She pointed to her own mouth then his. "Kiss."

"Ggggrrisss," he rumbled.

"Close enough," she allowed, trying to move past him.

He caught her and struck the exact pose the actor had, right down to Charles' brief, dramatic pause as the music came up, then Ra'kur brought his mouth to hers.

Even though he clearly had no idea what to do, just having his lips pressed to hers, breathing in his wonderful cinnamon scent, sent every nerve of her body alight.

She blinked up at him as he drew away.

He jerked his chin at her a little, his growl very soft. "Ggggrrisss."

Jenna searched his vivid blue eyes then, wetting her lips, took his face in her hands and he willingly bent down. Tilting her head, she brought her mouth to his. His breath drew in sharply when she flicked her tongue at the seam between his lips.

Her tongue touched the inner part of his lip, then she deepened the kiss. His mouth had more of that sweet spice taste to it and her arms wound around his neck to bring him closer. His hands went to her waist, resting there lightly, and when she drew back to meet his gaze, his eyes were wide and stunned.

Jenna's brow creased. He looked like he'd just been hit with a brick.

"You okay?" she asked, not surprised to find her own voice breathless.

He blinked a few times and she saw him swallow. Then he caught her face gently between his hands. "Ggggrrisss."

He lightly rubbed his nose up one side of hers and down the other again.

That's what he was doing earlier? Alien-style kissing me?

Any other questions, and the power to form them, fled as he rubbed his nose against hers again and made the growling-purring rumble that went right through her breasts and down her belly to tingle between her legs.

This time, when he brought his nose down the other side, he caught her in a kiss and his purr-growl against her mouth set her on fire.

He took his time kissing her, his mouth sliding over hers, taking his time as his tongue explored, the cinnamon-sweet taste of him luscious. His hands traced her body, lingering for a moment on her buttocks to press her closer, and she felt him hard against her belly.

The thought that this was crazy, that they might not even have sex the same way, flittered through her mind then stumbling, clumsy with wanting, she pulled him into her bedroom.

He never stopped kissing her and the rumbling had her ready to go right then. She was already so aroused, so wet, if he'd been human she would be riding him already.

In moments he had her sweater over her head and her jeans off, leaving her clad now only in bra and panties. They were nothing special, both just plain black cotton, but his gaze was hot as it ran over her. His fingers traced over her skin beside the bra straps, then cupped her breasts in his large hands. Her nipples hardened, her breath quickening as his thumbs flicked across the peaks.

He slid the straps over her shoulders, pulling the bra down to uncover her, and his gaze softened as he regarded her bare breasts. Gently he cupped one, seeming fascinated by the pale globe cradled in his palm.

His hands dipped to her ribs and waist and he tugged on the bra, looking frustrated that it didn't simply come away. Jenna's hands came up to unfasten it just as he impatiently tore the fabric.

He sat on the bed to look at her breasts, his hands still at her waist. He gave her a hot, questioning look.

Jenna gave a quick, breathless nod. "Kiss."

His eyes darkened and he pulled her toward him. For a moment he leaned his face in the valley between her breasts, inhaling deeply. For an instant the thought of those fangs crossed her mind then he gently caught her nipple in his mouth. Jenna caught herself against his shoulders to keep herself upright as his tongue teased, the tone of his rumbling going deeper. He traced his tongue over to her other breast and kissed there too and Jenna's hands threaded through his hair to press him closer.

His hands were at her panties now, sliding them down, and he drew back to look at her dark thatch of hair. He caught her around the waist and swung her onto the bed, then positioned himself over her and spread her legs wider.

Jenna felt herself blush at the absorbed way he looked at her pussy. His fingers traced her slit and he glanced at her.

"Here," she said, using her fingers to spread her folds. She wet her finger with her mouth and traced her clit with small circles while he watched and then, after a few moments, rested his forefinger over hers to learn the rhythm. Jenna slid her finger from under his and very gently he stroked her with the same circular motion. Her eyes fell shut and her mouth parted as his fingers moved against her.

She caught his hand and he blinked at her, clearly worried he had done something wrong.

"Now here." She took his finger and pressed it to her opening, and catching hold of his hand, she helped him slide his finger inside.

His eyes went wide, his breathing quickening as she showed him how to work his finger inside her. She wet her lips and with some urging got two of his fingers against her.

He slid both inside, groaning.

"Anything you want to show me?" she asked with a quick meaningful glance at his crotch.

He clearly understood but with plain reluctance withdrew his fingers from her folds.

He undressed. The top seemed to be both jacket and shirt, since he didn't wear anything beneath it. His skin was several shades darker than hers all over so it was clearly his natural tone, not a tan. His heavily muscled chest had only the finest of hairs, his stomach a perfect eight-pack.

His pants came off next and Jenna's mouth went dry.

"Now that," she breathed, "is a beautiful cock."

He was fully aroused and gorgeously formed, both shaft and balls, and for a long moment she just looked at his jutting penis. He wasn't too different from a human; larger certainly, the skin darker and tinged red, and she could see veins under the skin. He had some natural moisture already glistening at the head and she had a craving to lick it off.

His eyes shut, his purr deepened when she wrapped her hand around him.

He was big enough that her fingers didn't quite touch and he immediately pressed his cock further into her hand. His eyes opened a little, staying half shut as he watched her stroke him, his lubrication increasing a bit to make it easier.

Suddenly he tensed and caught her hand, a fine tremble running through him, and she realized he'd stopped her just before she made him come.

His gaze was blue fire as he shifted to lie beside her. He rumbled, brushing her nose with his before bringing his mouth to hers just as he caught her clit lightly between his fingers. Jenna groaned at the sensation as he stroked her; his rumble seemed to increase the tightening in her pussy by a factor of ten, and his tongue flicked against hers.

Jenna was moving against him, her hands threaded through his long dark hair, trembling with how close she was to climax. He moved then to lay between her legs, poised over her, his heavy cock against the inside of her thigh.

His eyes met hers and very, very softly he growled.

In answer she took hold of him and placed the head of his penis against her opening; she laid her other hand at his hip and pressed him forward.

He held her gaze and his mouth parted in a moaning purr as he sank into her folds. It was fortunate he had such natural lubrication; at his size she was already stretched tight when he filled her.

He stayed there, his arms caging her, fully sheathed inside her, his body trembling against hers. His entrance had him pressing slow and hard against her clit and she was desperate for more. After a moment she reached down and pressed his hips back, urging him to pull out.

He didn't fight her but his brow creased. As soon as he was out but for the head of his cock, she urged him inside again and his expression melted to one of aroused understanding.

He caught the rhythm quickly, his big body arched over hers. He nuzzled against her neck and with his rumbling purr it took only three thrusts of that hot cock for Jenna to come.

She was shaking from it and her climax just seemed to drive him higher. Her toes clenched as he plunged, driving himself deeper as his speed quickened. He drummed against her as no human man could have and Jenna's mouth parted as another climax hit her. His rumbling deepened and he thrust once more then stiffened. His fangs flashed, his face taut in pleasure, and she felt him pulse inside her as he came.

His breath shuddering, he collapsed against her, his big body still quaking from release. Jenna wrapped her arms around him, breathing in the cinnamon-like scent of him, feeling the slickness of sweat, human and alien, between them. Jenna pushed the hair out of her eyes, struggling to catch her own breath from the strongest finish she'd ever had.

Misinterpreting her gasps, he held his weight off her and she felt a flash of disappointment when he pulled his big cock out.

Gingerly—worried about breaking the bed maybe?—he shifted then curled his body around hers, cradling her.

He cupped her face and growled soft and low.

Tears suddenly blurred her vision. "God, I really wish I could understand what you're saying."

His alien eyes searched hers for a moment before he took her hand and laid it against his chest. She could feel his heart still thumping under her palm.

"Jjjeeennnaaa," he growled. "Rrraaa'kkuurrr."

This was insane. She couldn't believe what had just happened. He wasn't even *human*.

"Ra'kur," she whispered. "Jenna."

He drew her closer, kissing her lightly, her face, her mouth, her eyelids. He nuzzled her too, his face pressed to her throat to inhale deeply, and it wasn't long before he started the rumbling-purr again . . .

FIVE

Ra'kur's eyes snapped opened to the pale gray light of morning, his body curled around the softness of his mate. The symphony of this alien world's scents filled his nostrils and he drew them in, seeking any threat to her.

The forest beasts he'd encountered yesterday were in the woods nearby this rough shelter again. With those great horns and their speed they would make for an exciting hunt but startled easily. They did not seem as if they would become aggressive when not provoked so he dismissed them.

He lay still, listening, sorting through the foreign scents, his eyes sharp to any shadow or movement, not about to endanger his mate by carelessness or inattention.

But the shelter seemed secure.

After a few moments Ra'kur relaxed and permitted himself the pleasure of just *looking* at her.

She was tiny, even for a female; not that he'd seen many in his lifetime. The Scourge had been designed to kill the females of his kind, but *she* was far lovelier than even those few that had survived that disease. Her body was milk pale, and her face and form, even her bones, seemed delicate, finely crafted by the All Mother. Her eyes, closed now, were an astonishing russet color with tiny flecks of golds and greens. He had never known such softness, never even imagined it in his harsh, wandering life. Between his fingers, her hair was alight with a thousand lights of red and gold shimmering along their dark strands.

He could still not believe his good fortune to find her unclaimed.

Her full pink mouth was parted in sleep and shadows of care showed beneath her eyes. He traced the faint scar that ran along the underside of her left forearm, from elbow to midway to her wrist. The injury must have happened in childhood; he wondered at the wound that had caused it and how she had come to be here, in this frozen, remote place, all alone.

He could smell the fading scent of another who had inhabited this shelter—a male, older. The tang of his illness still lingered. Ra'kur thought of the rough, flat image she'd held so lovingly the night before, the sorrow in her eyes, the grief.

A sire, then? Or grandsire perhaps?

Of course that didn't explain why she would be wandering the forest alone, unprotected and still unmated. She must have scores of suitors.

Ra'kur let his breath out. It didn't matter now. They were fools for not capturing her and he already had. He would fight off any who sought to take her from him and it would not be long before he took her and left this world.

He sighed, remembering the damage done to his ship, the gagging smell of burnt circuitry, the emergency landing on this planet. A blast from a Zerar vessel had blown the entire directional assembly and the wormhole he'd opened hurled him to this world instead.

He gave a faint smile as she sighed in her sleep.

Not that he was sorry.

Still, it meant days on this backward world to make repairs before he could take his mate back to the homeworld. He couldn't wait to show her his house and lands, to enfold her in the protection of his clan.

His arms tightened around her. With so very few females left Jenna would be valuable beyond imagination. He would need all his clanbrothers' might to keep her. Hir's enemies had achieved their goal with the horror of the Scourge they had unleashed: his kind was dying out. He was deeply grateful to have found a lifemate at last, even if they would never have offspring.

Jenna . . .

Such an alien nameword! He struggled to pronounce it even though his people had spent countless millennia as traders and languages came easily to him.

Well, *usually* they did, he thought, chagrined. *Hers* seemed to be made up of different tongues, as if her world had been invaded in waves, each conqueror adding rules and words till the whole thing was one illogical jumble.

It was frustrating to struggle so to talk with the one person in the galaxy he most wanted to communicate with. It would be much easier when he got her back to the ship for the linguistic implant.

He brushed his mouth against her skin, pressing his face to the spot where her neck and shoulder met to breathe in the sweetness of her, like cali flowers warmed by sunshine. She stirred, her pink-tipped breasts brushing against him, and he grinned, the mating growl starting as his penis hardened, already lubricating in anticipation of more coupling.

Well, we will make do for now . . .

Jenna woke to a soft rumbling purr and caught her breath at the wet heat as he caught the peak of her breast in his mouth. Automatically she softened against him, his fingers already at her clit and stroking her to readiness.

Her eyes fluttered open as he urged her legs wider. His eyes glowed eerie blue in the faint light of morning, his black hair curtained his face as he positioned his cock at her opening and held her gaze as he entered her.

Caught beneath him, she wrapped her arms around his neck as he slid inside her, his eyes half shut in pleasure, and his rumble-purr deepened, vibrating through her clit with every stroke.

He held her face between his hands, gently brushing his nose against hers. His mouth touched hers and a single flick of his tongue between her lips sent her crying out as she contracted hard around him.

He moved fast and deep then, rigid inside her. He bent his head, his mouth open and moist against her throat, his big body taut. Two more deep thrusts and he was pulsing inside her.

His body was heavy on hers as his rumbling faded, his breathing still fast as he drew back to look at her. A smile flittered across his face as she blinked up at him. He pressed a quick kiss to her mouth then moved beside her, cradling her against him again.

"Holy cow," she managed weakly. Between last night and this morning they'd had sex no fewer than six times and both had climaxed many more times than that. His stamina was amazing and she had the sudden thought that if she stayed here another five minutes or so, he'd be rumble-purring again.

He tried to hold her when she pulled away but she shook her head.

"Look, I don't know about your people but I need something to drink. And a shower. And *food.* "

Her legs were still shaking as she stood. The cold didn't seem to bother him as he sat up, still bare, but she was already shivering and he gave a wolfish grin at her hardened nipples.

She pulled her knee-length robe and sheepskin boots on and headed for the bathroom while he dressed. She shut the door behind her. The lock was busted, of course, but he'd figured out she was serious about wanting privacy in here.

She washed her hands, looking at herself in the mirror, the flush on her cheeks, the brightness in her eyes. This whole thing was absolutely crazy.

But whatever happens I'm not sorry, damn it.

Jenna smiled when she came out to the living room to find him already dressed and leaning against the wall, his arms crossed as he waited for her.

"I'm starved. Are you hungry?"

His fangs flashed with a grin. "*Hhunnrrgyyy.*"

He caught her in a hug then with a quick nose rub went into the bathroom as she headed to see what she had left in the kitchen. From his emphasis on the word and their activities last night and this morning she figured she'd better make it a *big* breakfast.

She pulled the electric grill and stirred together the pancake batter. She had plenty of syrup and—since he liked it so much—decided to fry up the last of the bacon and make a pan of scrambled eggs.

She started a pot of coffee and poured some juice for herself, already cooking when he joined her in the kitchen.

Of course it wasn't easy to get anything done with Ra'kur kissing and nuzzling her every time she got near him.

She waved him off, smiling. "You want breakfast, don't you? *Hungry*, right?"

He made a *snorf* sound. His electric eyes were alight with humor and he very deliberately folded his massive arms as if to show her he would keep his hands off—for now.

She was flipping a pancake when she caught him drinking her orange juice.

"Hey!" she protested with a laugh. "That's mine!"

He looked from her to the glass in his hand, blinking, then offered it to her.

"Hold on," she said. "Let me get these flipped or they'll burn, then I'll get you some."

She topped off her own cup and handed him a glass and the jug of Tropicana since he was probably going to finish the rest of the juice off anyway.

She warmed the maple syrup in the microwave. She had two pancakes, a piece of bacon, and some eggs and put the rest on two dinner plates in front of him.

"Here," she said, pouring the syrup generously over the pancakes. She cut them for him too and speared a big mouthful onto a fork to hold out to him.

His face lit up at his first taste. He remembered the bacon from last night of course and seemed to like his eggs scrambled just as much as he liked them in omelet form.

Jenna sipped her coffee and, plainly noticing she hadn't served him any, he gave a curious sniff in the direction of her mug.

"It's coffee. Do you want to try it?" she asked, offering her cup to him. "It doesn't have any sugar or milk."

He took a swallow and made such an extraordinary face that Jenna bit the inside of her cheek to keep from giggling. He looked like he was trying not to spit it out in disgust but didn't want to offend her.

"Drinking it black really is an acquired taste. Hold on."

She poured another cup, adding a generous amount of milk and sugar as he guzzled some orange juice.

He sniffed then took a small, cautious sip from the mug she gave him. He seemed to find it made this way a lot more palatable but it didn't look like it was going to be a favorite either.

He had polished off all the bacon and the nine eggs on his plate and was happily adding more maple syrup to his pancakes when his head suddenly came up and he snarled.

Jenna jumped at the sound, her coffee sloshing over her hand.

Ra'kur's eyes were fixed toward the living room, his fangs bared, and in the next moment he bumped the table as he stood, already striding that way.

Jenna put her cup down on the counter as she hurried after him. "What's the matter?"

He stood beside the picture window looking through the glass, using the curtains to conceal himself. His body was taut and tense, his hand resting on the weapon at his hip.

He gave a low, menacing growl and Jenna frowned. There was nothing out there but mountains and her SUV buried beneath last night's snowfall.

Then she heard it too; the faint sound of an automobile coming this way.

Her eyes widened as the sheriff's car came into sight, heading up the curved road right for the cabin.

"Oh, my God," she whispered.

Ra'kur narrowed his gaze at the approaching vehicle, his fangs bared in a snarl as he drew his weapon.

She yanked the curtains the rest of the way shut and grabbed Ra'kur's wrist. "You have to hide!"

In the next moment she found herself shoved behind him.

"Come on!" she urged, her hands on his back trying to push him toward the bedroom. She got in front of him, grabbing his wrist to pull him that way. "Oh, please, hurry!"

He looked angry now, growling at her in his own language, unmovable as a rock.

A glance through the opening between the curtains revealed the car had come to a stop next to her SUV. Sheriff Riley was a peaceful man in his late fifties and a good sort. Pap and Bill's dad had been army buddies and she knew that, while Bill Riley might never have fired his service revolver outside of the practice range, he was a crack-shot hunter.

If he caught sight of Ra'kur, all bared fangs and alien eyes, a weapon in his hand—

"You don't understand! And, holy hell, he won't either!" she cried, her voice cracking with panic. "Oh, please! He'll *kill* you!"

His face was hard and set and in desperation she grabbed his hand and put it over her pounding heart.

"Ra'kur. Jenna. Remember?" The car was idling outside, and as the engine cut off tears stung her eyes. "Well, there isn't going to be a Ra'kur and Jenna, if you don't fucking *hide*!"

Brow creased, he searched her face then glanced at the window.

"*Please!*"

His jaw tense, he let her lead him into the bedroom and she heard the front stairs creak just as Ra'kur stepped over the threshold.

"Shhh," she whispered, her finger to her lips. "Just stay here and be quiet. Quiet as a space mouse, okay?"

On impulse she snagged her car keys off his belt. Ra'kur looked outraged, ready to protest, and she covered his mouth with her hand to hush him.

Jenna startled at the heavy knock on the front door.

"Just a sec!" she called.

She held her finger to her lips again to Ra'kur, then held her palm up, praying he understood what that meant now. Ignoring his frustrated, burning alien gaze she shut the bedroom door.

Bill knocked again, louder this time.

Jenna drew a shaky breath and went to face the sheriff.

Six

"Hey there, Bill!" Jenna opened the door only part way, blocking most of what *was* open with her body. "Whatcha doing up this way?"

Bill's salt and pepper eyebrows rose. "Came to check on you. Sarah Jane said you called in a plane crash?"

She forced a laugh. "Yeah, I guess I . . ." She nodded out toward the woods. "But there wasn't anything out there after all. So it's okay!"

His glance slid past her to the interior of the cabin. "Okay."

"*Any*way!" she sang out. "Sorry I troubled y'all. I went through the woods, didn't see smoke or nothin'." She gave a shrug. "Must have been a tree falling. Done just startled me, is all."

Bill gave a slow nod and she knew his suspicion had just ratcheted up to high. "Coulda been."

"Right," Jenna said after a moment. "So if there's nothing else—?"

"Actually, I'd be much obliged to you for a cup of coffee." Bill indicated the snowy mountain behind him with a tilt of his head. "Awful cold this morning."

"Sure thing," she agreed, nodding. "You wait right here and I'll fetch you up some."

His hand shot out and caught the door before she could shut it.

"You mind if I come inside and warm up a spell, Jenna?" he asked smooth as silk even as he held the door open against her push. "Like I said—awful cold out here this morning."

"Well, I'm not dressed . . ." He wasn't going to buy that for a minute. Bill had seen her in a bikini out on the lake dozens of times over the years. Her robe and boots had her covered as anything.

"Tell you what," he offered. "How 'bout you let me in now, an' you can go throw something on while'n I drink my coffee?"

Her dad and Bill Riley had gone to school together. After her parents died he'd practically become an uncle. If she didn't let him in now, he'd *know* something was wrong.

"'Course." She had to keep herself from looking toward the bedroom door as she stepped back. "Come on in."

He gave her a smile but his glance was already darting about and his hand hovered near the gun holstered at his hip as he entered.

Shutting the front the door behind him, Jenna took a quick furtive look around the living room. The coffee table was still pushed out of place but she'd turned the TV off when she'd come out here this morning. Things looked pretty much like they always did.

Bill sniffed at the air. "You baking something?"

Jenna was about to shake her head but then she caught it too. The lingering scent of cinnamon.

And sex.

"Pancakes," she mumbled, her face hot. "I—I was making pancakes. How about that coffee?"

Halfway across the living room her stride faltered, as she remembered that Ra'kur's breakfast was still sitting on the kitchen table.

Two place settings? It would be plain as day she wasn't alone here and with Pap gone Bill would take it onto himself to scrutinize any new boyfriend she had.

If he knew there was a man in this house with her, Bill would want to meet him. And Bill Riley wouldn't be taking no for an answer either.

"Why don't you have a seat?" Jenna threw over her shoulder. Bill was looking around, his eyes sharp. "I'll be back in sec. You like it light and sweet, right?"

She pushed the swinging door to the kitchen closed behind her. She couldn't remember the last time she'd shut it and some of the paint flaked off the door when she did. From the cobwebs at the corner behind it had also been a long time since she'd remembered to clean there.

Great, Bill will see I'm an alien-lover and *a lousy housekeeper.*

She grabbed Ra'kur's dishes off the table and threw his partly eaten pancakes into the trash. Jenna had his mug in hand, ready to toss Ra'kur's coffee into the sink, when Bill pushed the swinging door open.

Bill's glance took in the room.

"Sorry." She forced a smile. "I got me a messy kitchen today."

"I seen worse. Thanks," Bill said, taking the mug from her.

"Oh, that's—!"

Bill paused, his eyebrows raised. "What?"

Yeah, that's what, *Jenna? The alien's cup o' joe?*

"I think"—she tucked her hair behind her ear—"I might have added too much milk."

Bill took a sip. "No, I think it's fine."

"Sure I can't get you a fresh one?" she managed, watching him take a deep draft of Ra'kur's coffee.

"Nope," Bill said, raising the mug a little in a toast. "Just perfect."

"Oh, good," she said weakly.

Bill took a seat at the table, his hands wrapped around the cup like he was settling in for a long chat. "So, you say you went out looking for the plane?"

"Yeah, but I didn't find anything."

Even as she said the words she realized Ra'kur had to have come here *somehow*.

God, there's a fucking spaceship out there!

Coming on the heels of that thought was the shocked realization that Ra'kur might not be alone. There could be dozens of his kind in the woods outside, spread through the mountains, heading for the town below—

No, that didn't feel right. Something in his eyes, the eagerness for contact, the struggle to communicate, told of a very lonely existence.

"Did—did anyone else?" she stammered. "Find anything? Or call about it, I mean?"

Bill shook his head. "Just you."

"Oh." Jenna shifted her weight. "Well then, what are you doing here?"

"You ain't been answering your phone."

She glanced toward the avocado green dial-up that had hung on the kitchen wall for just about forever. "I had the phone turned off."

"I meant your cell."

"I dropped—I mean, I must have dropped it yesterday. Fell right out of my pocket. Out in the woods."

"Sarah Jane left a bunch of messages for you last night."

Jenna blinked then gave a little smile. "You and Sarah Jane a thing, Bill?"

His face flushed. "I'm just saying she called you is all. Wanted to check up on you."

"Oh. Well, that was nice of her . . . and you. But, as you can see, I'm fine."

"We—a lot of people around here—been worried about you, Birdie."

Her throat tightened at hearing Pap's nickname for her and her hand went to the charm around her neck. "I appreciate that."

"I know losing him was hard." Bill tilted his head. "You doing okay?"

The SUV's keys felt heavy in her pocket. Twelve hours ago all she'd wanted to do was get ahold of them and make a run for it. Bill Riley, armed with a loaded gun, was sitting right here in her kitchen. All she had to do was tell him there was an intruder in the house, that some not-human was hiding in her bedroom, and Bill would rally to her defense.

She and Bill could go through the mudroom and walk out the back door. Bill would call it in and the place would be surrounded.

He was an alien, for God's sake.

He'd shot her, cuffed her to her bed, taken her keys to keep her from leaving.

So why the hell am I still here? What is this, some kind of goddamn Stockholm syndrome thing?

Jenna recalled how he'd held her hands yesterday, washing them as tenderly as one would bathe a beloved child. How he'd stroked her hair while she cried over Pap. How he'd solemnly growled their names, holding her palm over his heart, and later how he'd lain wide-eyed, naked and trembling in her arms, how he'd curled around her afterwards, cradling her against him.

Bill would try to kill him. And even if Ra'kur were only wounded, they would call someone: FBI or CIA or whatever secret government department was set up in case of alien encounter and they'd take him away.

They'd imprison him, study him, *hurt* him.

The washroom was off the kitchen. She could grab some clothes from the dryer to put on, walk out the front door with Bill like there was nothing wrong, climb into the SUV, and drive away. Just not say anything to Bill about Ra'kur or to Ra'kur about leaving. She'd come back in a few weeks, after she was sure he was gone.

Just walk away from this and not look back.

She swallowed hard. Somehow she knew how badly that would hurt him, enough he might rather have Bill kill him.

"As okay as I can be," she said hoarsely, then added: "I miss him like crazy."

Bill gave her a sad smile over his mug. "I know, Birdie. It's never going to go away, it just doesn't, but it will get easier."

If she wasn't going to tell anyone about Ra'kur, if she wasn't going to make a run for it, then she had to get Bill the hell out of here—and quick.

She straightened. "Listen, I got a lot of packing to get to. Maybe we could meet up at Dolly's Diner for lunch or something in a couple days? Talk some more then?"

Bill took another swallow of his coffee then put the mug down and stood. "Sounds good. Want me to help you find your phone?"

She had no clue where the vehicle or spaceship or *whatever* it was that brought Ra'kur here was but she sure couldn't risk Bill seeing it.

"No, I think I know where I might have dropped it. I'll get dressed and head out in a couple minutes." She took the car keys out of her pocket and held them up. "And if I can't find it or it doesn't work or something, I'll drive into town and get one of those pay-as-you-go ones."

Bill gave a nod. "You call me either way, okay? Let me have the new number or give me a ring so I know the old one works."

"Sure thing."

She followed him to the front door and risked a sideways glance at her still-shut bedroom door.

Bill opened the front door, letting a blast of cold air into the cabin.

"Bill, if you see Lester Mills, could you let him know I'm not going to be putting the place up for sale for a bit?" she asked. "Just if you see him over at Dolly's Diner or something. I'll give him a call later to let him know. Once I find my phone, of course." She wrapped her arms around herself against the chill and offered a half-shrug. "I just . . . I need some more time here."

He gave her a respectful nod. "If I see him, I'll let him know."

She locked the door behind him and waited, looking through a crack in the curtains as Bill got into his cruiser and called in. It seemed an eternity until he started the car and backed up. It wasn't until his cruiser was out of sight that she let herself breathe easy.

She hurried to open the bedroom door and gave a startled cry as a snarling blur leapt at her.

SEVEN

Ra'kur lifted her right off her feet, wrapping her in a bear hug, his face buried in her neck, and she could feel the trembling tension in his big body. She wound her arms around his neck and he nuzzled her throat, breathing in her scent as if it were the only thing in the universe that could comfort him.

"Yeah," she whispered, stroking his black hair. "I was really scared too."

He made a huffing sound and set her on her feet. He growled, his tone sharp, angry, his electric eyes and fangs flashing.

"Oh, let me guess." Jenna put her hands on her hips. "You're mad at me now *'cause* you were scared."

Ra'kur gestured toward the front door, growling in his own language.

She couldn't understand him of course but she was getting the gist just fine and she threw her hands out. "What do you want me to say? 'I'm sorry'? A family friend—one armed with a *gun*, may I point out?—just showed up at the door. I couldn't *not* let him in!"

He gave a snarl punctuated with finality and with heavy footfalls stalked off to the kitchen.

"Hey!" she cried, outraged. *Goddamn it, why do men always do that?* "You don't just get to walk off in the middle of this!"

She arrived in the kitchen just in time for his annoyed *snorf* at seeing the pancakes he hadn't finished in the trash, and then his gaze fell on his coffee cup. He picked it up and took a sniff.

He narrowed his eyes at her.

"Oh, come *on*! You didn't even *like*—Yeah! He drank your damned coffee! It's not like I *gave* it to him. Bill walked right in"—Jenna threw a wave at the swinging door and then at the cup Ra'kur held—"and there I was—holding a cup of coffee! Of *course* he thought it was for him, because no one else was supposed to *be* here!"

Ra'kur's nostrils flared. He put the cup in the sink and folded his arms to glower down at her.

She glared right back.

Then she bit the inside of her cheek.

Finally, Jenna put her hand to her mouth but it didn't do any good. She burst out laughing.

"Look at us; we're arguing and we can't even *talk* yet," she said, putting her face in her hands for a moment and then flinging her hair back. "I can't wait for the fights we'll have when we can actually understand each other."

He looked equal parts amused as if he caught the absurdity of the situation and offended as if he were still too mad to be conciliatory.

In the next moment he caught her face in his hands and rubbed his nose against hers. He caught her mouth in a light kiss but he didn't start that rumbling-purr again.

Maybe he was worried Bill would come back.

He touched his forehead to hers. "Sssttaayy mmeee."

She blinked. He hadn't said a sentence, even a simple two-word one like that one, before.

"What? What did you say?"

"Jenna." He held her face in his hands, his words rolling like soft thunder. "Stay *me*."

"I'm sorry, Ra'kur." She searched his eyes. "I don't understand what you're trying to say."

He took her hand and pressed her palm to over his heart. "Jenna. Ra'kur. Stay *me*."

"You're asking me to stay with you? Is that what you mean? Or you noticed that I *did* stay with you?"

His frustration was evident and he looked pretty discouraged.

"It's okay," she said quietly. "Jenna stay."

He gave a faint smile then, as if he knew this abbreviated language wasn't what she would use either.

"Sorry about your breakfast," she said with a nod toward the trash can. "Can you hold out until lunch? I need to grab a shower and try to find my phone."

He gave a regretful look at the lost pancakes but he let her lead him back to the bathroom. Ra'kur stuck his hand in the water when Jenna turned on the shower. He was busy spreading his fingers under the warm spray and missed her pulling off her boots and robe.

"'Scuse me," she said, sliding past him.

He blinked at her as she stepped into the shower, his blue eyes flaring with interest and desire. She pulled the curtain partway closed, allowing him to see without completely soaking the rest of the bathroom. Jenna stepped into the water and tilted her head back to let the shower wet her hair.

She couldn't help but smile at Ra'kur's longing expression and held out her hand to him. "Want to join me? Best get in while the water's good and hot."

He hesitated, then glanced at the water running over her breasts.

"Come on, you don't have any objection to getting wet, do you?"

He turned his head toward the door, sniffing, then threw her a hot smile.

"I guess that means Bill won't be paying us another visit," she said as he pulled his clothes off.

It was her first time seeing him like this, standing naked in the light of day. He was so beautifully male. He had to duck a little under the shower curtain but the ceiling over the shower was plenty high enough. She was now extra glad that when they made the addition to the house they'd kept the old-fashioned tub separate and added this large shower stall instead.

Still, there wasn't a ton of room in here once you added a seven-foot-tall alien to it.

He blinked against the spray coming off her shoulders. She urged him to switch places with her so his back was to the water instead. By reaching around him while he ducked she managed to get his hair wet using the blue plastic cup she sometimes used to hold homemade hair conditioners. He watched as she poured shampoo into her palm and rubbed it between her hands.

He bent obediently when she gestured so she could reach, his face close to hers as she washed his hair.

He was over a foot taller than she, heavily muscled, and all the while his alien eyes reflected innocent curiosity and complete trust. He held very still for her ministrations, closing his eyes briefly, and made a rumbling sound of pleasure as she massaged the shampoo into his scalp.

She rinsed his hair, careful to keep the soap out of his eyes and followed with conditioner just in the ends of his hair.

Jenna lathered up the soap. "Close your eyes."

He tilted his head and she held two fingers up toward her own eyes then closed them to demonstrate what she wanted. As soon as his eyes were shut she started soaping his face.

He tensed a bit when she first touched him but soon relaxed. His skin was smooth, the bones and ridges of his forehead very different from a human's, but his cheekbones and jaw felt similar. She still didn't feel any stubble on his face or neck. He had light hair on his chest and very little hair below.

Maybe they just don't get beards.

She rinsed his face and he shook his head a little, blinking against some of the spray in his eyes.

She moved with the soap over his neck and chest, over the taut muscles of his belly, and then, with a mischievous grin, lower still. He was already aroused and his gaze went hot, his rumbling starting even before she wrapped her fingers around his shaft. His mouth parted in a half-moan half-purr as she stroked him with soapy hands. His hands clasped her shoulders, his cock growing harder still in her grasp. He rumbled deeper, his breath picking up speed, and he pressed his shaft into her hands. She cupped him where he was soft and a few more strokes had him coming in hot spurts against her belly.

He was still gripping her shoulders, gasping with his release. She slid from under his hand and went on tiptoe to press a kiss to his mouth. He gave a clumsy nose rub in return and she noticed his legs were shaking. She got another lather and finished washing him, even his feet, an action that really had his expression delighted.

He caught her in a hug and dropped a kiss to her wet hair. Then with an absorbed, focused expression he repaid her in kind.

He copied her actions, massaging the shampoo into her scalp and carefully shielding her eyes to keep any soap from getting into them while he rinsed. Ra'kur washed her face exactly as she had his, even lightly exploring the bones of her face as she did, careful to rinse her face with water as she had his before moving lower. Slippery with soap his hands ran over her breasts and dipped into her waist. Urging her legs apart, he washed there too and after a moment Jenna caught his hand.

"Let's get rid of the soap first," she said breathlessly and when she'd rinsed his hands urged him back to what he'd been doing. His fingers were at her cleft, already stroking her, and Jenna closed her eyes.

He bent, his cheek touching hers, his soft rumbling sound against her ear sending her arousal soaring and his fingers quickening their light strokes against her clit to inhuman speed. Her mouth parted at the sensation and his arm went around her waist to support her just as her knees went weak. Jenna was holding onto his shoulders, hovering just at the edge when he turned his head and very gently nipped at her neck. The feel of those sharp teeth lightly scraping her skin caught her by surprise and sent her soaring into climax.

Her breath was still coming fast when she opened her eyes, her trembling hand going to that spot where her neck and shoulder met. He hadn't broken the skin or bruised her, but he seemed to have an instinctual sense of what she needed, and when, to make her come.

She blinked up at him and his look of male pride faded a bit.

He searched her face. "Okay?" he growled.

She nodded. Her body was still tingling and heavy with pleasure. Sex with him was the absolute best and she didn't even know what had her so freaked.

He wrapped his arms around her, holding her against his chest, and tears stung her eyes because now she knew. Before, she'd been biding her time to escape. Last night she couldn't help but throw herself into the experience, but in the back of her mind she was going to get away from him.

But now I don't want to get away at all. And there's no future for us.

Ra'kur gave a soft, soothing growl, stroking her back with his broad palm.

She swallowed hard and seized on what kept her going during the long days of Pap's illness.

No use dwelling on what's coming, make the most of now.

"I'm okay," she said and let herself relax in his embrace.

With tender care he finished bathing her, even bending to wash one foot then the other. She shut off the shower and before she could reach for one he had her wrapped in a towel and was using another one to dry her face, arms, and legs.

His enthusiastic rubbing of her hair had her laughing and backing away before he could make the dark tresses into a complete tangled mess.

When he was dressed again and she was clad in jeans, T-shirt, and sweater he watched while she used the hairdryer on her hair.

His hair was shaggy, nearly to his waist, and she wondered if his people didn't cut it or he just hadn't bothered to.

"I used to cut Pap's hair. I could trim yours," she said, holding up the scissors. She ran her fingers through the still damp ends of his hair, and pantomimed the action. "Just a little bit, maybe just to clean up the very ends here?"

Ra'kur's cheeks flushed and, dropping his gaze, he gave a short nod.

He was so tall and his hair long enough she didn't even have him sit while she cut. The conditioner had made the strands soft, so black it shone blue as she ran her fingers though it. In all she'd only cut about an inch off but she thought it looked much better as she pulled away the towel that she'd used to protect his shoulders from the falling hair.

He'd stayed still, almost shy, as she'd cut but his body tensed when she started to dry his hair.

She thumbed the dryer off and cupped her hand over her ear as if trying to block sound.

"Is it too loud for you?" She switched the setting to low. "Better?"

He gave a relieved nod and she was mindful to keep the dryer away from his ears as much as possible.

One thing he especially liked was using the brush on her hair. He brushed and brushed, rumbling happily as he smoothed her long locks.

"I think that's plenty," she teased and he looked disappointed when she took the brush from him.

He followed her out into the living room. She debated whether to start another log burning now—the ancient furnace could use all the help it could get—or to wait till they came back from the phone search.

"What 'Jenna'?" he growled.

Her brow creased. "That's my name, remember?" She pointed to herself. "Jenna."

His hair caught the light with his sharp headshake. "What '*Jenna*'?"

"I don't understand. 'Jenna' is me."

"Ra'kur." He tapped his chest, then curled his huge hand into a fist. "*Strong*."

"Oh, you mean what does my name *mean*?"

He jerked his chin at her. "What Jenna *mean*?"

"What *does* Jenna mean?" she corrected automatically. "Pap said it meant 'little bird.' That's why he called me 'Birdie.'"

He blinked.

"Okay, way too many new words at once there." She held her forefinger and thumb close. "Little." She held up the gold charm that Pap had given her. "Bird. Little bird."

"*Little bird*." He cupped her cheek with his hand and his alien eyes shone. "*Mine* little bird. *Jenna*."

Her vision blurred. For all its simplicity she'd never in her life heard such a heartfelt declaration from anyone.

He jerked his chin at her. "Water-eyes."

"Yeah, guess you took me by surprise there," she said with a shaky laugh. "It was nice though."

He searched her face. "Water-eyes?"

"Because of what you said."

His brow creased. "Water-eyes *name*."

"Oh! You're asking about my *tears*." She pointed to her eye. "When humans' eyes have water that's called 'tears.' When I'm sad or hurt I have tears."

"Sad?" He looked upset. "Hurt?"

Jenna waved her hand. "Or happy."

He gave her a look that said exactly what he thought about her having a reaction that could mean any, or all, of the three.

"Actually, since we're on the names subject, what *are* you? I'm human. Bill, remember him?" she asked with a wave toward the front door. "He's human." She picked up the case for the movie they'd watched last night and pointed to the photo. "Charles and Nell are *human*. What are you?"

He gave a short, clipped growl.

"Greehaar?" she tried.

He shook his head and repeated the word. She tried twice more and he seemed pretty satisfied with her third attempt of "grah-here."

"How did you come here? To this world?" She realized she was waving her arms around in a way that could probably mean anything. "Wait, I have an idea. Come on."

Jenna pulled on her down jacket and zipped it up. He was in front of her as soon as she opened the front door, already scanning the woods and sniffing.

After a moment he gave her a nod and she stepped out onto the porch.

"There's nothing up here," she said, heading down the stairs. "Sometimes you see a black bear and there's been some wolves but even they're rare. Your worst worry is snakes or coming up on a hornets' nest cause they sometimes build them in the ground but that's not gonna happen in winter. Now *this* is my SUV," she continued with a gesture at it. "Which I really need to clear the snow off of. Man, that's going to be a pain now," she muttered, giving the ice crusted over the snow a disgusted push with her gloved fingers. "Anyway, this is my car. It takes me from place to place." She pointed at the tire tracks Bill's cruiser had left behind. "That was Bill's car. What do you have? Where is it?"

In the sunlight reflecting off the snow he was both handsome and alien to her eyes now. His eyes glowed inhumanly but she recognized the intelligence, humor, and warmth in their blue depths now.

Was it only yesterday that I was terrified of him?

He jerked his chin toward the woods in the direction she'd searched. "There," he rumbled.

"Will you show me?" She pointed at her eyes then in the direction he'd indicated. "Show me."

He gave a short nod. "Will show you, Jenna."

She blinked. "Wow, you're picking up English fast. My language is called 'English.'"

"Human language is *English*," he repeated.

"Uh, no. *My* language is English. Other humans have other languages."

He frowned. "Much languages?"

She recalled her sociology textbook in college said there was an insane number of languages—some with a very low number of speakers, of course—currently spoken on Earth, something like six thousand.

"Yeah, but I only know one." She'd taken a couple years of French but she could barely remember how to ask directions to the ladies' so that didn't count.

"I have much languages," he said. "English is a pain."

"*What?*"

His alien eyes were puzzled. "To take snow from car— *a pain*. English is a pain."

"Yeah, I did say that, didn't I?" Jenna shook her head. "Do you remember"—she touched his temple—"everything I say? All my words?"

Ra'kur looked surprised. "Yeah."

She gave a short laugh. "That should be 'yes.' And a better word for 'a pain' is 'difficult.'"

"Yes," he echoed, a growling rumble rolling his words. "English is *difficult*."

"Yes." She was hyperconscious of her slang and diction now that she knew he was absorbing everything like a sponge. "English is difficult, even for humans to learn."

In his eyes there was a glimmer of amusement and the frustration of not being able to share his humor, the questions he wanted to ask and sorrow at lacking the ability to do so.

She felt it keenly too, the longing to be closer, to share.

He caught her hand in his and in silence they continued down the mountain. Ra'kur led her to the place near the creek where she'd been so spooked yesterday.

"Uh, I don't see anything," she said, frowning.

He let go of her hand and took two steps forward. He raised a finger and tapped the air. In response the woods seemed to shimmer for a moment and revealed—just for an instant—a long oval shape.

Jenna's mouth parted. "How the hell do you do that?"

The spaceship was disguised—cloaked somehow—so well that she'd stood right next to it yesterday without knowing. Sure, if she'd tried to take a few steps closer or tried to get to the other side of the creek she would have walked right into it. And like yesterday the ground looked just like mud.

"The spaceship would have been hot from entering the atmosphere," she murmured. "I smelled something but with everything so wet from the snow . . ."

Jenna took a step forward and tapped as he had. The outline of the ship shimmered for an instant then vanished.

"Why isn't there snow on it now?" she asked. "It snowed last night so there should be snow all over it, right?"

He looked ready to speak then glanced at where the ship would be if she could see it. He looked frustrated and shook his head. "No snow."

So there was an explanation but he just didn't have the language skills to convey it.

And he's learning English a hell of a lot faster than I could ever hope to pick up those growls of his.

"Can I see the inside?" She pointed to her eyes. "Will you show me the inside?"

In response he waved his hand. There was a hissing sound and from where she stood she could see a doorway in front of him.

And still no spaceship around it.

He took a step forward—and vanished.

Jenna drew her breath at his sudden disappearance. She hurried to where he had been to see the doorway in front of her, and Ra'kur just inside.

It was so unreal—to see the woods around the doorway and Ra'kur standing inside a room too. It was if he had opened a magic door smack dab in the middle of the North Carolina woods. But this wasn't magic. It was an illusion created by a superior technology and she suppressed a shiver.

How much more advanced *were* his people?

He held his hand out to her. "Show you, Jenna."

She wet her lips and clasping his hand, stepped inside.

EIGHT

The interior of her very first spaceship wasn't the shiny silvery wonder she'd expected. It was metallic but had a dark, worn feeling to it and the lights that illuminated this squared-off space were a warm yellow shade. The floor looked scuffed and a bit like he'd tracked mud in that had dried. There was another door with a window and what looked like sealed supply closets on either side.

"So, this is the foyer, huh?" she asked, joking from nerves. "Coat closet, place to dry the umbrella?"

He glanced around the space as if trying to understand her comments by looking. He tilted his head at her.

She waved it away. "Sorry, just kidding."

She couldn't see anything through the interior window except total darkness. Suddenly all those ugly stories about alien abductions and hideous medical experiments flashed through her mind. Movies featuring powerful beings with superior technology and no mercy—

"Okay, Jenna?" Ra'kur searched her face, his rippled brow creased.

He wouldn't hurt me. Ra'kur would never *hurt me. Like Pap would say, not for all the tea in China.*

"I'm okay." She let her breath out. "All right, so show me the rest."

There was a keypad next to the door with sixteen keys and symbols. He tapped a code into the keypad, the light over the door went white, and the door slid open.

Immediately the interior lights came up. There was a corridor that went off in either direction. It smelled a bit like singed machinery and cinnamon.

It was warm inside, enough so that Jenna pulled off her gloves, stuffed them in her pocket, and unzipped her coat.

He nodded to the corridor to the left. "Here."

He led the way. At various junctures were lit panels—controls of some kind—and Ra'kur gave each a cursory glance as they went by. He keyed open another door and Jenna caught her breath to see the curved windows showing the woods.

"The cockpit, right?"

There were two seats at the front near the controls and two set higher up and behind.

Guess you'd call those the back seat.

Jenna shrugged out of her jacket and put it across one of the seats. She laid her hand on the headrest; it felt smooth, like leather.

"Are there more like you, Ra'kur? Other g'hirs here?"

His shaggy hair showed blue highlights with his sharp headshake. "No others."

She frowned at the way he said that. "Are there any others? At all?"

He held his fingers close together. "Little."

"You're alone?"

"No more." His gaze softened, his alien eyes lit from within. "Jenna stay me."

Her eyes stung.

"Hurt?" He cupped her cheek, examining her face worriedly. "Sad, Jenna?"

She didn't know. "Happy."

And sad.

Because whatever she felt—whatever *this* was—didn't have a chance in hell.

She blinked the tears away. "Hey, come on, this my first spaceship ever. Show me the rest, okay?"

She longed to explore the alien spices and flavors in the galley he led her to, wishing she could ask him about it all. Next to the galley was a room with a table and four chairs fixed to the floor. Couches lined the next room and everything big was attached to the floor. Everything in here would be a comfortable fit for him and oversized for her.

He had a sleeping room with a large bed, one wide and long enough for even him to stretch out, and there were two other sleeping rooms being used for storage. There were other storage rooms as well and the last room he brought her to had an antiseptic smell to it.

"Infirmary," she guessed from the set-up of the room. The thought of it brought her up short. "What happens if you get sick or hurt, Ra'kur? Who takes care of you?"

He regarded her with frustrated eyes. He took her hand in his.

"Give names," he said earnestly. "Here. Please."

Jenna shook her head. "I don't understand."

He opened one of the drawers and took out a cylindrical metal instrument. It was about eight inches long and he gripped it tightly as he held it out to her. "Give names, here. Please."

He brought the instrument up and she flinched back, bringing her arm up defensively.

"What are you doing?" she cried.

He stopped short. Moving slower now he lifted the instrument to her eye level. He brought the thing toward his neck and pantomimed the act of pressing it against his skin. "Give names."

"Ra'kur, I'm sorry. I really don't understand." Jenna looked at the instrument warily as she lowered her arm. "What is that thing? Can you tell me another way?"

"*Tell,* Jenna!" He threw his arm wide to indicate the room and by extension the spaceship around them. "Ra'kur not have *English!*"

"Language," she breathed. "You can't learn my language fast enough to tell me everything you need to." She looked at the instrument in his hand. "Will that let you understand English somehow?"

He nodded, holding up the instrument again. "Ra'kur will have English. Jenna will have mine names."

"So I let you do this then you'll know my language and I'll know yours?"

"Yes." He touched her temple then his. "Will know *language.*"

Jenna wet her lips. If she did this she would be able to understand him, finally be able to talk to him. Some of the sounds he made seemed like they were going to be flat out impossible for the human tongue to mimic. He was tons better at her language than she was at his but he was still struggling. It might be months or years before they could communicate well.

And God, the opportunity to talk to an alien was fantastic but the truth was Jenna just wanted desperately to talk to *Ra'kur*.

She glanced at the instrument in his hand. "Is it going to hurt?"

He looked regretful and she took that to mean, yeah, it's gonna hurt.

"Okay." She gave a nod, her hands clenching into fists like they always did at the dentist's office. "Go ahead."

Captured

As he raised the instrument to hold it to her neck, a thousand questions that she *should* have asked before agreeing to this flashed through her mind. Like, what if something goes wrong with it? How will you get it out? *Can* you get it out? How can injecting me with something teach anybody a new language anyway?

But he already had the thing against her neck, behind her right ear. Before she could stop him to ask some of those questions she heard a hissing sound and gasped against what felt like the worst combination brain-freeze and migraine of her life.

Ra'kur made soft, soothing growls as her hands came up to her temples in an effort to keep her head from exploding. She was struggling to keep her breathing even, trying not to throw up as Ra'kur stroked her hair.

She groaned and pressed her hands harder against the sides of her head as the pain grew worse. "God, that fucking *hurts!*"

"—stand me?"

Jenna brought her throbbing head up. "What?"

Ra'kur leaned forward, his bright eyes anxious. "Can you understand me now?"

He was still growling; she could hear the growling but in her head she heard *words.*

"Oh, wow," she breathed. "That's *weird.*"

Ra'kur searched her face worriedly. "Little bird, can you understand me?"

She pushed her hair away from her face. "Yeah, I can understand you."

"Are you still in pain?"

The throbbing was starting to fade. "It's getting better now."

He let his breath out. "Thank the All Mother. It should not have hurt you so much."

"The 'All Mother'?"

He tilted his head. "What do you call the giver of all life?"

"Uh, Pap was an agnostic but he liked some of the eastern stuff, like Buddhism." Ra'kur was looking at her blankly. "Okay, I'd say 'God.'" She gave a short, choked laugh. "We're talking. We're actually talking. You're speaking your language and I'm speaking mine and we're *talking*."

He smiled back. "There has been so much I wanted to say to you. But first I must thank you for your courage, for your trust."

Jenna thought about falling on her butt in the snow, screaming her head off as she tried to get away from him yesterday. "Yeah, I don't think I'd call myself 'courageous.'"

"You let me place the linguistic implant."

"*That's* what you injected?"

"Of course." He looked puzzled. "You said humans had many languages. You must have similar devices."

"No, we don't have anything like this."

"How can you speak to one another?"

"Well, some people grow up speaking more than one language and others learn as—Can we get back to whatever you just injected me with?"

He touched the base of her skull. "Is it malfunctioning? I can understand you."

"No, it's working fine but *how* is it working?"

"It attaches to the language center of your brain. The chip transmits the translation directly."

She stared. "I have an alien chip in my *brain*?"

"Yes."

"Uh, okay," she said after a moment. "I guess I'm the only one here who has a problem with this."

His brow creased instantly and he lifted the instrument again. "Does it still pain you? Do you feel dizzy?"

"I mean the *concept* of—Wait, what would you do if it did still hurt?"

"I would remove it."

"But then I wouldn't be able to talk to you."

"I would learn English." His fingers brushed her cheek. "I would never let you hurt if I could help it. I would do anything to keep you from hurting."

"It's okay," she assured him. "It doesn't hurt anymore."

He put the instrument down and took her hands in his. "There is so much I want to know about you." He gave a short laugh. "I want to know everything."

"I want to know about you too. Like, where are you from?"

"A world very far from here."

"You probably don't need to dumb it down quite so much," she said, a little annoyed. "I'm not stupid."

His face flushed. "I do not think you are stupid but your world is very primitive. I am not sure you will understand."

"So just ignorant then?" And it stung a bit on account of he was probably right but she had inherited Pap's pride along with his brown eyes. "Try me."

"My world is called Hir. It is the fourth planet of the Sarion system, sector twelve."

"Oh." After a moment she blew her breath out. "Okay, no, I don't know where that is."

He smiled. "There is no reason you should. My people have never come this far."

"You said there were few g'hir now." He'd actually said "little," but she took that to be "few." "What did you mean?"

His face clouded. "The g'hir are dying."

Her grip tightened on his hands. "You're dying?"

"No, my *kind* is," he said roughly. "The Scourge is killing us."

"The Scourge? What's that?"

"Biological warfare." His eyes flashed. "The war was nearly at an end. The Zerar cities were destroyed, their military smashed, they were days from defeat." Hate sharpened his features. "Then they unleashed the Scourge on us."

"Wait, it's a disease?"

"A hideous one, designed to kill our souls along with our kind," he said hoarsely, looking at her hands in his. "It kills only females."

She should be ashamed for feeling this way but Jenna's shoulders fell in relief. "So men don't catch it?"

"No," he snarled. "We were left untouched, left to watch our females die. Our mothers, our clansisters, lifemates, daughters. I cannot tell you what it means to one of us, who have such instinct to protect . . ." She saw him swallow. "Few survived. Perhaps one female in five hundred did. Now the g'hir are dying out."

"That should be enough, shouldn't it?" she asked, frowning. "To rebuild your species over time?"

"Not all that survived were young. Or left fertile."

Oh, man . . .

"How long have you been alone, Ra'kur?" she asked quietly.

His eyes were haunted. "The Scourge first came to our outer colonies when I was eight summers. In weeks half our population was dead. Our society was destroyed, our warriors shattered. None of the females of my blood survived."

"I'm sorry." She'd lost Pap but he'd had a good, long life. She couldn't imagine what it would be like to lose so many.

"As soon as I could I began searching. I have been searching for years."

"Searching?" Jenna asked. "For what?"

"You," Ra'kur growled softly, cupping her cheek. "My little bird. My lifemate."

"What?" she blurted.

"Lifemate." He tilted his head. "A female I have mate-bonded to."

"Mate-bonded." She gave a nod. "Okay, sure. Mate-bonded."

"You cannot say you do not remember." He gave a short laugh. "You *chose* me."

"I did?"

His brow creased a little. "I captured you. You took drink from me. You let me feed you."

Jenna blinked. "So all you had to do is give me something to eat and drink? What about the sex?"

He grinned. "That too."

"*That's* why you shot me?"

"I gave you ample time to run away if you did not find me a desirable mate." He searched her face and his brow creased. "I thought you wished to make it easy for me."

"I *was* running away. And in case you haven't noticed, I move a lot slower than you do."

"You did not wish to be captured? Was that not a mating cry you made?"

"A mating—? Uh, no, that's called *screaming* and humans do that when we're frightened."

"You were frightened?" His frown deepened. "Of what?"

"Are you *kidding*? How about a huge alien coming out of nowhere and roaring at me?"

"I invited you to mate with me!" he exclaimed, affronted.

"*That* was a mating call?"

"How do human males invite a female to mate?"

"Well, in college it's 'what's your major'?' Then it's 'so, what do you do?'" Ra'kur's frown deepened and Jenna waved it off. "Never mind. In any case, he'd come up and just talk to me."

"Then ask you to mate?"

"Not right off, not without getting his face slapped. Maybe he'd tell me I'm pretty."

"I *did*," he said impatiently. "Why else would I make a mating call to you?"

She blinked. "You think I'm pretty?"

His expression was caught between frustration and disbelief. "You are beautiful." His face clouded again. "I fear you are too beautiful."

He really seemed to mean that. She was okay-looking but no raving beauty for God's sake. Jenna ducked her head. "I can't tell if that's a compliment or not."

"It is fact. You are delicate, lovely." His glance went over her. "And your female scent is very arousing."

"Oh." Jenna's cheeks went hot. "Thanks . . . I think."

His gaze met hers. "You are embarrassed."

"Sometimes human men say things about the way a woman smells that are—uh, not very complimentary."

He paused, thoughtful. "Then human males have a very poor sense of smell."

"I've been wondering about that—Just how good is yours?"

He took a light sniff at her. "You are fertile now."

He was right, she was between her periods and she shut her eyes briefly. "Can we talk about something that doesn't have to do with my intimate anatomy? Like—could you hear Bill coming or smell him first?"

"Bill?" The translator implant thing was working but when he said the name it sounded like an angry snarl. "The male who entered our shelter today?"

"Yeah, Bill, the sheriff."

"What is 'sheriff'? This is not a word in Hironian."

"That's your language? Hironian?" He gave a nod and she continued, "A sheriff is someone who enforces the law. Bill's a sheriff."

"This male is a peacekeeper?"

"That sounds about right. So, smell or heard? Which was it?"

He considered. "Heard. Then the foul scent of the vehicle, then the smell of the peacekeeper and a female's sex scent on him."

She giggled. *Wow, way to go, Sarah Jane.*

"I'm sorry," she said in response to Ra'kur's confused look. "I didn't realize he and Sarah Jane were together 'til he slipped a bit talking this morning. Bill would be absolutely mortified if he knew anyone could *smell* that they'd been having sex."

"How could any not know he has a lifemate? It is obvious."

"He and Sarah Jane aren't, uh, lifemates. They're just dating."

"What is that?"

"Dating?" She shrugged. "You know, like dinner and a movie and stuff. Spending time together, to see if you like one another enough to take it further."

"I smelled the female's sex scent on him," he insisted. "They must be mate-bonded."

Houston, we have a problem . . . "Ra'kur, people can have sex without being lifemates."

His sharp glance went over her. "There was no male's scent on you."

"I bet there wasn't." She pushed her hair back. "It's been a long time."

His gaze narrowed. "You have had sex with a human male, Jenna?"

"Yes, of course I have."

He sure looked put out now.

Hey, sauce for the goose is sauce for the gander, pal. Jenna folded her arms. "Have *you* had sex with a g'hir female?"

"No," he growled, his tone chilly.

Idiot! Of course he hasn't. Not if most of them are dead, if they died while he was so young. But that would mean . . .

His wide, seeking gaze the first time, the eager clumsiness when he entered her, how he needed her cues to learn how to thrust—

Oh, my God.

She wet her lips. "Ra'kur, have you had sex with anyone?"

"I have mated with you," he said, his growl sharp, hurt.

"So . . . I was your first?"

His glowing alien eyes were raw. "First," he said hoarsely. "Only. Forever."

"Oh," she breathed.

He turned away. "I have to fix the ship."

NINE

"Fix it?" Jenna followed him back into the corridor. "What's wrong with it?"

"The Zerar weapons blew out the directional assembly. If I cannot fix it there is no way home."

"The Zerar?" she cried. "They're still around? I thought you said the war was almost over."

"They are rebuilding while the Scourge brings my own people to ruin."

"Ra'kur!" She caught his arm. "Is there any chance the Zerar could come here?"

His fangs flashed. "I will *never* allow anyone to hurt you!"

"I wasn't—I mean, my world, Earth. Are we in danger from the Zerar?"

"*Everyone* is in danger from the Zerar," he snarled. "They are monsters; demons who must be wiped from existence!"

Jenna felt herself blanch and his expression softened.

"I do not think they will come here," he said. "It was an accident that I did. The directional assembly was damaged and the jump brought me here instead. Your world is far from our area of space. I was surprised the wormhole I generated could have brought me to so distant a place."

"That's how you travel? You open a wormhole?" She was pleased it came out sounding like she had the slightest idea what she was talking about. "So . . . so this ship opens a kind of doorway in space from one place to another and you just fly through? But couldn't they do that too?"

"It is not an easy thing to do; it takes a great deal of power to travel this far. I was fired upon in the moment I opened the wormhole. Instead of jumping to Hir's orbit, I arrived here. Almost before I understood what had happened I hit your world's atmosphere. I was lucky to land at all."

"But the only thing wrong with your ship is that assembly thing is broken?"

Just the thought of him leaving made her feel a little panicky and a wicked, selfish thought wormed into her mind.

What if he can't go home? What if he has to stay here—with me?

And then . . .what? Take him to Dolly's Diner and introduce him around Brittle Bridge as my boyfriend? Take day trips into Asheville to check out the new art exhibits? Hit the farmers market come summer and spend days sitting on the porch and eating strawberry pie with the town alien?

He couldn't stay here. If anyone found out about him the government would take him away and wipe out all evidence he had ever existed. They would take her away too. Sex with an alien? She'd be a lab rat as quick as he. Even if they got to the media and went public before the government found out, people would fear him, hate him.

And he couldn't spend a lifetime hiding in the cabin.

He *had* to leave. As soon as he could.

Don't think about it, just don't, just like Pap, 'cause if I do I'll fall apart and I have to be strong.

"Yes, but I cannot open a wormhole until it is repaired and the ship has only enough power left to make a single jump now. No," he corrected, "I *can* open a wormhole but I will not be able to control where it opens and that would be far worse."

"Okay, what do you need to fix it?"

"I do not know," he admitted. "I have not examined it yet."

"You haven't even looked at it?" Man, that'd be the first thing she did if she found herself stuck on some strange world.

"I intended to. I was in the cockpit, happy to have landed at all, dismayed to find myself in this frozen place, on this alien world and then"—his eyes shone—"I saw you."

"Oh." She couldn't help a little smile, then she remembered something. "Wait a minute. Why did you handcuff me?"

"Do *what*?"

She held her wrist up, her finger and thumb touching around it. "The cuffs. Why did you handcuff me?"

"To prove I was a warrior worthy of you. To show that I could capture any prey, even you." When she didn't respond, he said impatiently, "If you did not find me a desirable mate, you should have taken them off."

"I *was* trying to take them off!" He looked hurt and she ducked her head. "And of course I wanted you. I mean, jeez, you *know* that I do."

His fingers went under her chin to tilt her face up. "I am grateful for the gift of your human kiss. It is very arousing."

"I like the nose rubbing too." She could feel herself flush. "And that rumbling sound you make."

He took a step closer. "It is to ready your opening for coupling and heighten your experience."

"Well, it does the job," she mumbled. "And *how*."

He traced her lower lip with the tip of his finger. "I want so much to pleasure you now." He gave a frustrated half-groan. "But I cannot ignore my responsibilities. Allow me to examine the assembly and determine the needed repairs . . ." He bent down to brush his mouth against hers, the softest of rumble-purrs tightening her center. "And I will bring you to your pleasure until you beg me to stop."

"That might take a while." Jenna teased, a bit breathless now. "You know, I actually wore out one of those rabbit things once."

His brow creased. "Rabbit things?"

"Probably don't eve have vibrators on your world; I can't imagine a woman ever *needing* one." He looked mystified and she patted his chest. "Come on, let's get a look at the assembly thing before I try to wear you out too."

An hour later Ra'kur gave an annoyed growl and pushed away from the open panel. He'd bent over the machinery with the silent focus of one well accustomed to solitude and it made her wonder what his life had been like, flying around alone in this thing for years.

"Well?" she asked. "What's wrong with it?"

"The calibration matrix is fused," he grumbled. "I must fashion a new one."

"I hope you have the parts you need to do that onboard," she said, concerned. "It's not like Andy's Hardware in town is going to stock them."

"I can take parts from other ship's systems to use." He passed his hand over his eyes. "But then I must alter *those* systems so that they will function as well."

"But you can make the repairs with what you have on hand?"

"Yes." He sighed. "But the repairs will take days."

"That's not so bad." She would have days more with him, maybe even a whole week before the thing was fixed. Before he had to go. "And it's not like I'm gonna kick you off my land."

His head came up. "Your land?"

"Yeah, this property is mine. Pap left it to me."

"You are owner of all these woodlands, Jenna?"

"Yep. Five hundred acres of North Carolina mountain that no one can walk on without my say-so."

He jerked his chin toward her. "What of the horned beasts?"

"You mean deer? On white-tailed deer only the males have horns; they're called bucks. Well, it's my land to hunt too. But I'm not much of a hunter. In fact, hypocrite that I am, I'll eat meat but killing things turns my stomach."

His chest puffed up. "I am a skilled hunter," he growled. "I will slay a beast for you."

"I guess that would be okay," she hedged, already trying to think of how she'd even get it to Ted Baker, the guy who used to process deer for Pap. "As long as no one saw you. No other humans anyway."

"Show me the boundaries of your lands. I will hunt only within them."

"Oh, uh, sure." She glanced at the panel. "You mean after you've fixed this?"

His shoulders fell a little. "Yes, my first responsibility is to repair the ship."

"Well, I have to get out there and find my phone," Jenna said, standing. "If you'll show me how to leave."

He got to his feet. "We will find your device."

"You can stay here and work," she offered. "I'm pretty sure I know where I dropped it. Though after a whole day in the snow I don't know if it'll still work. Let me just go grab my coat."

He was waiting by the door to the outside when she got back from the cockpit. She didn't have a hard time finding her way around, as it was logically laid out and all in all wasn't a big spaceship.

She couldn't imagine spending years on it, alone . . .

She zipped up her coat and pulling on her gloves noticed that he was checking his weapon.

"Really, you don't have to go with me, Ra'kur. It looks like you've got tons to do."

"You must not venture out unaccompanied." He holstered the gun. "I will seal the ship again and then we will search."

Jenna's eyebrows rose. "You know, it's not like I'm going to get lost. This is my land, my world, remember? I spent half my life running around these woods. I know them like the back of my hand."

"And I will go to protect you."

"I don't need you to protect me. I can take care of myself just fine."

A wounded look flashed in his eyes and his jaw hardened. "I will do so even if you do not *need* me."

Damn it, she hadn't meant to hurt him. "Okay, fine," she muttered. "You can help me look for my phone."

He gave a short nod and tapped the keypad to open the first door.

"Why are there two doors?" she asked, looking around the foyer-like area.

"Airlock," he said, closing the interior door and opening the one to the outside.

Guess that makes sense.

She was about to head out when he put his hand up to stop her. His eyes scanned the woods and he breathed in. After a moment he stepped outside and continued his evaluation of the area.

Finally, he gave a nod and stood aside to allow her out. In the next instant the doorway and any evidence of the ship vanished again.

"Thanks," she grumbled, her boots crunching in the snow as she threaded her way through the trees. "I meant what I said before. Your worst worries out here are hornets and snakes and this time of year you don't have to worry about them either. Maybe there's the occasional wolf and you sure don't wanna come across a mama bear and her babies, but the cubs are only being born about now."

"With you I must always be alert."

Jenna threw him a glare over her shoulder. "Because I'm so helpless?"

"Because you are so precious."

That brought her up short. His alien eyes were stormy, his jaw tense.

"Thank you," she said, her voice softer and a whole lot more gracious this time. "That was really sweet."

"It is true," he said roughly. "You are my heart, Jenna. You are my life."

And pretty soon you're going to have to go away forever too . . .

"Hey, look," she said, forcing a bright tone and heading for the rough path that led up the hill to the house. The trees were thick around this little area and the cabin far enough away you couldn't see it from here. "This is where we met. Me screaming my head off, ready to brain you with a heavy branch and you trying to tell me alien-style you thought I was hot." She paused, considering. "You know, sadly, it's not even the worst first date I've ever had."

"*Brain* me?"

"I intended to defend myself by bashing in the skull of whatever jumped at me. Didn't you see me wielding the tree limb?" she asked, poking around in the snow with her foot for her cell.

"You were my prey." His luminescent eyes met hers across the clearing. "I watched everything you did."

"Yeah, *that* didn't come out creepy at all." She put her gloved hands on her hips. For such a small area it was going to be a lot of ground to search for a cell probably buried under three inches of snow now. "Did you happen to see where I dropped my phone?"

His eyes scanned the snow-covered ground and she saw his nostrils twitch. Suddenly his gaze sharpened and he took a few steps to the right and knelt. He brushed aside snow with his long fingers, a gentle action in someone so massive, to reveal her cell.

"Wow," she murmured as he handed the phone to her. It was almost out of a charge but it looked like it had survived all right. "You must be a *very* good hunter."

He turned his head to look east. "There are three beasts that way. A female and two males."

"Probably a doe and two of her fawns from last year." Jenna glanced in that direction. She couldn't even see them. "You can smell them from here?"

"Yes. I saw such beasts flee yesterday. They will be challenging to catch."

"*Catch?* You mean you'd *run* after one of them?"

He gave a feral grin. "It will be an exciting hunt."

Bucks could run thirty-five miles an hour but with Ra'kur's speed he might actually be able to run one down.

The whole idea of being with someone who had that much power gave her a chill.

"You are frightened." His sharp gaze swept the woods then rested on her again. "Why?"

"It's just"—Jenna shifted her feet—"you're so much stronger than I am. So much faster, your vision and sense of smell is much better than mine. I couldn't hide from you—or outrun you—in a million years."

"Why would you *want* to?" he asked, baffled.

She wet her lips. "It's just—you being so much stronger . . . I feel at a disadvantage."

His brow creased. "All of what I am as a warrior is meant to serve you. I will run to bring down a beast to feed you by my own hand. My sharp sight will detect threats to you. My strength will keep you safe."

"Some men—human men—use their strength against women." Jenna gripped the cell in her hand. "Sometimes they hurt them."

He started to shake his head and then his eyes widened. "Has this happened to you, Jenna?"

She looked away.

"Little bird?"

She turned, heading back to the cabin. "I need to charge my phone."

In an instant he was there, blocking her retreat, his brow furrowed.

"Look," she said, her eyes on his chest. "The whole thing was awful. I didn't even tell Pap everything. I don't even like to *think* about it."

Ra'kur sank into that otherworldly stillness of his, patient as the mountain itself.

And just as unmovable.

She shut her eyes for a moment. "There was this guy in college . . ." she said, her voice low, reluctant. "Ricky. He was gorgeous and funny and charming; I couldn't believe he was interested in me. And at first, I thought everything was great. But there were . . . little things, stuff that was easy to ignore—him not liking movies I chose or restaurants I'd picked. He didn't like my friends, complained they were trying to split us up 'til I just stopped seeing them to avoid a fight. He was always putting down whatever I did or liked or wanted, then he'd say he was kidding, that I was too sensitive. He had a quick as fire temper too and I never knew what would set him off. Sometimes when I'd make a mistake he'd call me stupid." She dropped her gaze, looking at his boots now. "I just couldn't take it anymore and when I told him how I felt, he just discounted everything I was saying. I told him I wanted to break up and it got ugly. We were both yelling by then and he . . . he threw me against the wall. Next thing I knew he had his hands around my throat."

She swallowed hard. "I was so scared. I thought he was going to kill me. I fought back hard and ran outta there as soon as I got loose. The cops took a report but nothing came of it and the university wouldn't do shit. Even after I broke up with him, he followed me around, called me in the middle of the night, said he was going to make me sorry, that I deserved whatever he did to me. He told everybody I was crazy and they fucking believed *him*." She shook her head. "Oh my God, I was a mess. Jumpy all the time, couldn't sleep, couldn't eat, afraid to go anywhere. I was so embarrassed, so ashamed. I'm *still* ashamed . . ." She pushed her hair out of her face. "I kept wondering what I'd done to make all this happen. I had to withdraw from school mid-semester and transfer to a new college to get away from him."

Ra'kur had stayed very still as she spoke but she could detect a faint tremble to his muscles now.

His fangs bared, his whole face savage. "Tell me where this male is. I will kill him."

"No." His expression was outraged and Jenna sighed. "Even if I knew where he was—and, thank God, I don't—I wouldn't tell you. Yeah, he's an asshole and he should be stopped, punished, *whatever,* but I wouldn't put you at risk for what happened four years ago. And I was lucky that I *did* get away from him. I mean, I just kept ignoring what my gut was telling me and by the time I admitted to myself how wrong things were I didn't have any friends. I couldn't bring myself to go to a therapist. Of course one of them would have seen it all before—the explosion, the sweetie-I'm-sorry roses time, then pretty soon the hurting and humiliating starts again. I know lots of women stay with men like that 'cause they think it's going to get better, 'cause they get torn down and they don't have anyone else or any money to go, 'cause they're afraid if they leave the guy will kill them . . ."

"Jenna," he growled softly. "Do you fear me?"

She studied his face and listened to her gut. It was funny to remember how alien and frightening he seemed just a day ago. "No. No, I don't."

He let his breath out. "I am glad of it. I would never hurt you." He cupped her cheek, his hand very warm despite the chill. "But I am g'hir and I cannot be other than I am. I sought you under a thousand stars and seeking you gave meaning to my life. I *must* be permitted to protect you, to provide for you, or I would find my life unbearable."

She raised her chin. "I won't let you boss me around."

He smiled faintly. "Even I do not possess such courage."

Her eyes narrowed and he caught her hands in his, his expression solemn.

"Do you trust me, little bird?"

The truth was he was already a hell of a lot stronger than she was and it sounded like everything he'd done yesterday was in keeping with the way his people did things.

"Yes, Ra'kur," she said softly. "I do trust you."

"Then trust I do not seek to rule over you." He touched his forehead to hers. "But only to safeguard the gift the All Mother has blessed me with. For me, to do less would be sacrilege. To protect our mates, to honor our women, was always a sacred trust. But now, in the wake of the Scourge—you cannot begin to imagine what a female, *every* female, means to us now. To harm one is unpardonable, a crime against the Goddess herself."

"Okay," she breathed. "Okay."

He bent his head to rub his nose against hers then brushed a kiss against her mouth.

He drew back to look at her. "You are so beautiful, my Jenna."

The light reflecting from the snow softened his features, his blue-black hair and rippled brow. "You are too."

He laughed, his fangs flashing. "Males are not beautiful."

"*I* think you're beautiful." She gave his hands a squeeze. "And there's no use arguing with me."

His eyes crinkled with humor and he inclined his head. "If it pleases you to think so."

She raised her eyebrows. "You know, I was real patient while you were fixing that panel."

"You were," he agreed.

"You promised if I let you look at that panel," she reminded, sliding her arms around his waist, "you'd leave me begging . . ."

TEN

Looking into her decimated pantry, Jenna blew a lock of hair that had escaped her ponytail off her face. The fridge was nearly empty too. She was lucky she could cobble together their lunch and even with her culinary skills she wasn't sure she had enough to make dinner tonight.

Every morning after breakfast they went to his ship and he'd set pillows out for her so she could sit nearby comfortably and talk with him as he worked. The repairs were going well, but slowly on account of them stopping so often to get tangled up together in his bed. They came back up here, holding hands as they walked through her woods, for lunch and supper and spent the evenings snug together in the cabin. She liked showing off her cooking for him—fried chicken and gravy, biscuits and chocolate cake—as much as he enjoyed polishing it all off.

And in the past three days she'd learned just how expensive it was going to be to keep a seven-foot-tall alien warrior well fed.

'Course it was all worth it for the look on that warrior's face as he sampled his very first root beer float.

Ra'kur sat at the battered kitchen table, his huge hands wrapped around the frosty glass, straw in his mouth, rumbling happily as he started on his third float.

"I wish to have more of these," he said with a blissful look at the foamy contents of his glass. "I will have them with every meal."

"Yeah, I'll need to hit the Harris Teeter if we're going to have any meals at all." She gave a final look at the empty pantry and shut the cabinet door. It probably hadn't been this bare since the Great Depression. "In fact, I don't even need to make a list because we're out of *everything*."

"Harristeeeeterrrr?"

"It's a grocery store," she said, dusting her palms against her white cook's apron. "It's where I buy food."

His straw made a slurping sound as he finished off the last of his float. He put the glass down and gave a nod. "We may go now."

"Uh, no. Ra'kur, you can't go with me."

"My repairs are nearly completed." He leaned back in his chair and with a practiced eye checked his weapon, then holstered it again. "An hour's work at the most remains."

"Ra'kur," she began slowly. "We've talked about this. There aren't any people on this world who aren't human. You can't go into town. You can't let anyone see you, I told you that."

His brow creased. "I did not think you meant *never* let anyone see me."

"What did you think I meant?"

He glanced at her breasts, her body. "I thought you were shy about letting others know that we have been fucking so much."

Jenna crossed her arms over her chest, her back against the pantry door. "You know, maybe we could try another word for that?"

"Bashful?" he offered.

She closed her eyes briefly. "I meant instead of 'fucking.'"

"But that is what we do." Ra'kur frowned again. "We fuck."

He was right and, really, it was just how the linguistic chip managed to translate it, but it still got under her skin that he called it that.

"So your people never call it 'making love'?" she asked, annoyed at how important this suddenly was to her. "It's always just 'fucking'?"

His face lit up. "I like this new way of describing how we fuck."

"You know," Jenna said, rubbing her forehead, "maybe we tackle that later and get back to the 'not-letting-anyone-see-the-alien' part."

"I will not let you go unprotected." Ra'kur stood, seven feet of brawn, glowing eyes, and bared fangs. "I am going with you."

"You *can't*." She took quick steps to stand in front of him. "If anyone sees you they'll—I don't know—panic? Or call out the National Guard or something!"

"I will not let you go about alone on a planet so uncivilized as this."

"Wait a—did you just call my home, my world, *uncivilized*?"

"Jenna," he began, and his growl had an overly patient tone that set her teeth on edge. "This is an unsafe world for females. You have told me so yourself. I will not allow my lifemate to put herself in danger to purchase foodstuffs. I am going with you."

"Do you know what they would do if they found out about you?" she demanded, throwing her arms wide. "If—and that's a big *if*—they didn't kill you on sight, they would capture you, experiment on you—!"

"Perhaps," he growled, "because they are *uncivilized*."

Her eyes narrowed at having proved his point for him.

"Ra'kur," she began, willing herself to an even tone as she took off her apron and laid it over the back of the chair. "I'm going into town. You can work on your ship or take a nap or watch a movie, *whatever*—I'll be back in about two hours."

His jaw hardened. "I am going with you, little bird."

"No, you're not!"

"Then you will not go." He folded his arms, looking down at her from his great height. "And we will make do with the provisions I have on my ship."

Jenna put her hand on her hip. "Just how many provisions do you have out there? Because, quite frankly, you could out-eat a whole football team."

"It would be pleasant to have more human food," he allowed. "But we do not need it in any case. We will leave in a few hours' time."

Jenna blinked. "Leave? What do you mean, 'we'll leave'?"

"Leave," he repeated. "Journey to my homeworld."

"Well, you just . . .?" The thrill that he wanted her with him smashed against the realization that in his mind her *leaving the fucking planet* was up to him to decide. "Don't you think you're *assuming* a little here?"

"I am not assuming. I have reconstructed the directional assembly and need only recalibrate the system. Once that is done we will gather your possessions and leave this world."

She took a step back. "I'm not leaving. I'm not going *anywhere*!"

"Of course you are. You will return with me to Hir."

"Just when did you decide that?" she demanded.

He frowned. "The first time we fucked."

"And you didn't even stop to think that maybe you should *ask* me?"

"We are lifemated, Jenna," he said sharply. "You *must* come home with me."

"*This* is my home." She backed away further, shaking her head. "And I'm not leaving it. I'm sure as hell not going to another planet!"

His eerie inhuman eyes narrowed. "You are being unreasonable."

"*What?*" she flared. "What did you just call me?"

"Even if I were welcome here by other humans, you cannot truly expect that I would allow you to continue to live on this—"

He broke off, snapping his head toward the living room and baring his fangs, his whole body taut.

Her breath caught at the sudden change. "Ra'kur?"

"Trespasser," he rumbled. "The peacekeeper has returned."

"Bill's here?"

She'd called and left Bill a message three days ago, as soon as her phone had charged. What the hell was he doing here?

"Okay." Jenna headed for the living room, scrambling to think. "Okay. Hide. I'll find out what he wants."

"I will not *hide*," Ra'kur snarled, stalking after her.

"You hid the last time he was here!" she threw back. "What the hell was so different then?"

"I knew little of the ways of this world and you were so frightened I thought it best to comply then."

"Yeah, and I'm frightened now, goddamn it!" she cried. Sure enough, that was Bill's cruiser coming up the road. She urged Ra'kur toward her bedroom. "Don't you understand? He *can't* see you!"

"I do not care if he sees me! If he shows himself a threat, I will kill him."

She felt herself blanch. "Stop it," she whispered hoarsely. "Don't even talk like that."

Ra'kur's huge hands clenched. "I have every right to defend my lifemate!"

Jenna wet her lips. Bill would be knocking on the door any second. Ra'kur wasn't human, he was a g'hir warrior and he was reacting as if Bill really were a danger to her. But nothing could be further from the truth; somehow she had to get him to understand that—and fast.

Ra'kur's alien visage was fierce, savage.

Deadly.

"Bill was my father's friend," she said, keeping her voice quiet and even. "He was my grandfather's friend. He's like an uncle to me. The last time he came here it was because he'd tried to contact me and got worried when he couldn't. Bill is a good man, a man who would protect me with his life if I had need of it." She touched his arm, felt the trembling tension in his muscles. "You want me to trust you. Well, right now, I need you to trust me. Please, Ra'kur, hide."

His nostrils flared but at last he gave a reluctant nod. "I do not like this. I will be vigilant. I will come if you have need of me."

"I won't," she promised. "He'd never hurt me."

With a final unhappy look Ra'kur went into the bedroom and eased the door shut.

"Hey, Bill," she said cheerfully but not like the manic cheerleader as she had last time as she opened the door for him. "Good to see you. Everything all right?"

Bill gave her a long-suffering look. "You ain't been answering your phone again, Birdie."

She frowned. "You've been calling me?"

She glanced back to see the phone where she'd left it on the coffee table. A few steps and she had the cell in her hand.

"Damn it," she muttered. She held it up to show Bill. "I forgot to tell you. The cabin and the back woods are some kind of dead zone for this thing. I have to go out front to get reception."

"Now, Birdie, what kinda phone is gonna be any good if it don't work in the house?" he scolded. "Lester Mills's been calling you, Sarah Jane's called you, and now I'm driving up here to check on you again. It ain't right for you to be needlessly worrying folks who care about you."

Jenna kept her eyes on Bill but she could swear she heard a very soft agreeing *snorf* from behind the bedroom door.

I didn't even get one of those damned floats.

"You're right and I'm sure sorry," she said in her most conciliatory tone. "I promise to go outside and check for messages at least once a day."

Bill held up a finger. "You need to either get yourself the house phone cut back on or you get your butt to town and get a cell that'll work up here."

Jenna gave a nod. "Yes, sir."

Bill held her with a narrow look for a moment. "All right, then," he said, straightening. "You come on outside now and show me that thing works."

Jenna kept her eyes off the bedroom door but her heart sped up. Would Ra'kur consider this threatening?

"It works," she promised. "It works just fine if it's got reception."

Bill stuck his tongue in his cheek for a moment. "In fact, I'm gonna stand there and make sure you hear all them messages." He indicated the stairs behind him. "Get your coat, Birdie, and let's go."

She hesitated, the cell gripped in her now sweaty palm.

"Well, come on, girl!" Bill said, stepping back. "You got your foot nailed to the floor or somethin'? I ain't got all day—let's go!"

"Okay," she said, a little too loudly. "I'll just come outside for a minute, just to show you my phone works, Bill, then you can get back to town. I know you can't stay long."

Jenna grabbed her coat. In the sliver of light under the bedroom door the shadows shifted restlessly.

She stepped outside with Bill and shut the front door behind her.

ELEVEN

"See?" Jenna asked, ending the call to her voicemail. "I got 'em all."

Bill blew out between pursed lips, his breath showing in the cold. "All right, then." He gave her a stern look. "Now, next time I see Lester and Sarah Jane they'd best tell me they got a call from you, saying as to how sorry you are they was frettin' on you."

"So, Bill," she called after him as he headed for the cruiser. "How long you think it'll be before you'll be seeing Sarah Jane to ask her that?"

His cheeks reddened. "You mind your business, Jenna McNally, and keep a civil tongue in your head."

"Don't I always?"

Bill shot her a sour look then gestured at her SUV. "And get that thing cleaned off case you need it in a hurry."

She frowned. "Why would I need it in a hurry?"

He paused at the car door; the worry lines clear on his face now. "Last night at Dolly's Chester Davis said he saw something a couple days ago near his property, running fast. I said, Ches, it weren't nothin' but a damn bear, and he said it didn't run like no bear. Said it didn't growl like one neither."

Damn it, I shouldn't have let Ra'kur run the land like that, even at night!

But he'd needed so badly to blow off some steam from the long hours of working on his ship. There'd been a full moon that evening, the air cold and clear as could be, and he'd been just itching to show her how fast he was. Graceful for all his size, his speed was breathtaking and she'd lost sight of him in moments as he took off toward the woods. Even hindered by snow she'd bet he could run down a buck without breaking a sweat. He was flushed when he returned to her, grinning with pride at her wide-eyed admiration. His deep rumbling laugh echoed through the woods as he swung her into his arms to carry her inside to their bed—

It was January; black bears would be hibernating now. Bill knew that too.

"You know Chester done always drink like a fish," Jenna said with a toss of her hair. "He musta seen a bobcat. Or a wolf, maybe."

"You seen anything?"

"No, sir."

"I guess if'n you can't be bothered to take two steps from the house to check your messages, Birdie," he grumbled, "then you sure as hell ain't seen nothing out here."

Jenna kept her expression contrite, knowing anything she said back to that would likely just come out sounding like she was sassing him.

Bill sighed. "All right," he said, sounding a bit weary. "You take care now."

She gave a nod. "You too."

She waited outside while Bill got in the car and waved as he pulled away. As soon as the sheriff's car was out of sight the front door opened behind her.

"I guess you heard everything," she said. He'd probably be able to tell her what her heart rate had been.

"I think he is, as you say, an honorable male." Ra'kur came to stand beside her. "I am glad I decided not to kill him."

Jenna's head snapped around and he gave a deep, rumbling laugh.

"Oh, *very* funny," she muttered.

"You do not appreciate my joke, little one," he teased and dropped a kiss on the top of her head.

"Yeah, that whole 'aliens slaughtering my friends' humor is positively wasted on me."

"Come." He caught her hand and urged her along toward the woods, to the path they'd walked so many times before. "I must finish the ship's repairs and take you home where you will be safe."

And that brought them right back to the argument they were having when Bill showed up.

"Ra'kur, I can't just move to another planet."

"Hir is a very beautiful world and not so different from this one," he said, their boots crunching the snow. "There is nothing to fear."

"I'm not afraid," she protested as they passed into shadow, the trees growing denser around them. Not true at all; she just wasn't sure whether she was more afraid of going with him or how it would feel when he went without her. "I—I can't just leave Earth."

"You will come home with me, Jenna." He gave her hand a gentle squeeze. "You will live at my clan's enclosure. I will keep you safe and you will be happy there."

"Enclosure?"

"Like your woods," he answered with a nod at the forest around them as they headed down the hill. "The Erah clan has much land, many of my blood live there."

"You still have family there?" she asked, surprised.

He gave a faint, faraway smile. "Yes, though it has been very long since I have seen my father, my brothers, or even spoken with them. It was difficult, sometimes dangerous, to contact them while I searched."

"You have brothers? Older or younger?"

"Both are younger. I had two sisters as well." His face clouded. "Before the Scourge took them and my mother."

"I'm sorry," Jenna said quietly as the trees gave way to the clearing where they'd met.

He stopped in their little clearing, his face ragged in the winter light. "I was only eight summers when the sickness came to our enclosure. In three days all the females of our clan were dead or dying. The ground trembled with the keening of warriors. Some did not survive their loss." She saw him swallow. "I wonder at it still that my sire did. But he is clanfather and so many needed him to live."

"Clanfather?"

"The Erah's leader, but like most enclosures we have no clanmother now."

"It's hard for me to imagine." She shook her head. "Half the population just wiped out like that."

"No, it was far crueler than that. Had the illness taken half our people that would have injured us but to tear our females away as they did—They cut the very heart from our kind and left us in agony." He focused on her again, and his eyes softened. "And you, my Jenna? There are no others of your blood now?"

"No, not now that Pap's gone. My parents and Becca—my big sister—they were all killed in the car wreck. That's how I came to live with him."

His fingers traced her cheek. "I am so glad you were not with them."

"I was actually. I was only six so I don't remember much. Highway patrol said that when the back window smashed I got thrown free. I got cut up a bit, not bad, but I broke my arm. Pap"—she swallowed hard, fingering her necklace—"he gave me this when he came to get me from the hospital and said, 'Cain't nobody take the place of your momma and daddy but you got me, Birdie, always. And I'm gonna make sure you don't want for nothing.' I told him how grateful I was, before he passed, for all he had done for me. And he said"—tears blurred her vision—"he said *he* was grateful on account that raising me gave him a whole bunch of joy."

Ra'kur pressed a kiss to her forehead. "You will bring joy to our enclosure too, my Jenna, when the clan welcomes you."

He turned, his hand taking hers again as he headed toward the creek to the place where his ship remained cloaked.

"Would they welcome me?" she asked. "I'm human. Wouldn't they object if you brought an"—funny to think of *herself* this way—"alien home?"

He gave a deep laugh and opened the door to his ship. "No, I will be much envied." His gaze fell on her again and he sobered. "But we must go directly to the enclosure when we arrive on Hir. I cannot risk any others seeing you."

Not that she was actually going to go but— "Because I'm human?"

"Because you are so beautiful." His mouth curved into a rueful smile. "Many warriors will seek to take you from me."

"What do you mean, take me from you?"

"Kill me." He gave a careless shrug as they stepped inside and the door slid shut. "And claim you for themselves."

"*What?*"

He raised black eyebrows. "I do not fault them for this. I would fight and kill to take you from another. I will do so to keep you."

"Thanks," she managed. "I think."

He turned to key in the code to open the inside door. "No one will ever take you away from me. My clanbrothers will help me keep you."

"Ra'kur"—she caught his arm—"I can't just go live on another planet."

"There is no more need to talk of this," he growled. "This is the way it will be. This is the way it *must* be."

She stared up at him, at his set jaw and shuttered alien eyes.

She let him go and took a step back.

"Well, I guess I just don't see it that way," she said quietly.

She'd been in the ship often enough to know how to open the outside door herself. She stepped through and headed back up to the cabin.

"Would you have us live *here*?"

She glanced back down the hill to see him following. He threw his arm out to indicate Pap's woods, making a dismissive wave at where she'd spent most of the happiest times of her childhood, of her life, of the clearing where they'd met.

"On this primitive world? Where you so fear that someone will see one not of your kind that you hide your own lifemate?"

"You didn't even *ask* me if I wanted to spend my life with you," she threw back at him, plodding up the slope. "You just decided that's how things were going to be!"

She gasped; she'd scarcely heard him move behind her before he caught hold of her arm. He was just so goddamn *fast*.

"How can you say such things to me?" he demanded. "I called to you. I offered my life in service to you. I offered my body for your comfort and protection!"

Jenna looked away. "Humans do things differently, Ra'kur."

His breath caught and he went very still. "Are you saying you do not want me as your lifemate?"

She wasn't being fair and she knew it. He'd done everything the right way according to his species, his culture.

"I don't know what I want," she mumbled and pulled her arm out of his grasp.

She trudged toward the cabin, her eyes on the snow-covered ground, knowing he followed her, knowing there was no hope of compromise on this.

She just *couldn't*. If she went with him, she might never see home again.

She was already well past the tree line when a metallic squeak brought her head up.

Bill, just now turning away from the front door where he'd been knocking, spotted her from his place on the porch.

"Hey, Birdie!" he called, waving as the screen door shut behind him. "I clean forgot to tell you that Lester—"

Bill broke off, looking past her, his face going slack in shocked disbelief.

Ra'kur was only a few paces behind her, already out of the woods, clear as day.

Oh dear God . . .

They'd been inside the ship—that must be why he hadn't heard the car. Bill's scent had to be strong here from his earlier visit and Ra'kur distracted by their arguing or he would have noticed Bill had come back.

Bill went for his sidearm and Ra'kur's snarl ripped through the air.

"Birdie!" Bill shouted, taking aim. "Get down!"

"No!" She darted to the side to throw her arms out protectively in front of Ra'kur. "Bill, don't—!"

A crack echoed across the mountain. Bill's eyes were fixed on her, the gun trembling in his hand, his mouth working as Ra'kur skidded to a stop beside her.

Jenna's brow creased. Her body felt funny, heavy, as if a great weight was pressing down on her shoulders. Scalding pain suddenly burned through her upper chest and she blinked down as red spread across the front of her white jacket.

"Jenna . . ." Ra'kur whispered.

She lifted her head to meet his wide gaze. "I think—"

Her legs gave out.

"No!" He fell to his knees in the snow to catch her against him. His black hair curtained his face as he cradled her, the brilliant sky behind him pale in comparison to his eyes.

She wanted to hold him too but her arms wouldn't work.

But she could hear everything—the faint bubbling when she tried to breathe, Ra'kur's heart thumping in his chest, Bill's gun click as the barrel turned, the sharp, high call of a cardinal in the woods—

"Go home . . . I . . ." This was really, really important but she couldn't get a breath, her vision darkened at the edges. ". . . Ra'kur, I . . ."

"Stay with me, Jenna. You promised." He held her tighter. "You *promised*!"

Blackness took her. The last thing she heard was Ra'kur's roar and the shrill sound of human screams.

TWELVE

Someone was keening.

The long mournful sound went on and on, dragging Jenna upward toward consciousness. She fought it, that pull, knowing that at the other end lay pain and fear and confusion.

But she knew the voice making that agonized plaint; she could feel his suffering in the very cells of her body.

Ra'kur.

She grabbed hold of that wail and let it take her then, lift her upwards, let it carry her toward him.

The strange antiseptic smell hit her first. It smelled like hospitals always do but odd too and she wrinkled her nose against it. There was the familiar feel of a mattress beneath her, a pillow under her head, a blanket covering her, and the dull burn of an IV in her arm.

It took a huge effort to open her eyes, way more than it should have. For a moment Jenna could only lay there, the whole of her concentration committed to keeping her eyes open, to staying here with the light and hurt and weakness.

Ra'kur's head was bent and he sat beside her bed, rocking, his shaggy black hair showing blue highlights as he swayed.

She tried to swallow past the god-awful dryness in her mouth. Her lips felt cracked and her gaze darted around the room. This wasn't part of his ship—that was for sure. The walls were a soothing light brown, the ceiling white, and everything else—equipment and furniture alike—had a pristine shiny look to it that his ship didn't. Bewildered, she saw a running display on the wall over her bed. Trying to read the three-dimensional alien language as it scrolled by made her woozy.

His shoulders were shaking and while g'hir didn't cry like humans did, she knew they felt things just as deeply. She reached toward him and found even her best effort only moved her hand a spare inch.

"Wha—" she breathed.

His head shot up. There were shadows under his eyes, his face was drawn; he looked utterly exhausted. "Jenna?"

"What . . ." She tried swallowing again, past the agony of dryness in her throat. "Happened?"

"Jenna?" He blinked rapidly. "You are awake? You are awake!" He caught her hand, holding it between his big warm rough ones. "They said you would never—!" He turned toward the door and bellowed: "Healer!"

Jenna winced, squeezing her eyes shut against his roar.

"Stay awake, little bird," he pleaded. His hand touched her forehead. "You must stay awake!"

She forced her eyes open to meet his anxious gaze.

"Water," she croaked.

He let go of her hand then to fumble at the table beside her. Jenna let her heavy eyes fall shut.

"Honored warrior," another g'hir said sharply, his words deep growling sounds like Ra'kur's, although she could understand him as perfectly as if he spoke English. "I am sorry for your loss but—"

"She is awake!"

"Warrior," the man began gently. "Your lifemate is not going to—"

Jenna opened her eyes and managed to turn her face toward the speaker. He was g'hir too, not nearly as tall or burly as Ra'kur but with the same ridges on his brow, the same heavy eyebrows and inhuman face.

It was funny really how she'd never stopped to think about it, assuming that all the g'hir would have dark hair like Ra'kur's, but this man was blond. His clothes were different certainly—instead of a warrior's dark brown leather he wore a medium blue outfit that strongly resembled scrubs. His glowing eyes were green, not blue, and they widened as they met hers.

His glance flew to the scrolling display over her head. "This is not possible! She cannot have regained consciousness!"

Doctors! Jenna turned her head toward the straw Ra'kur held toward her mouth. She took a long pull and closed her eyes in relief as the blessedly cold water hit the back of her parched throat.

"Wait! She should be examined before she is given liquids orally!"

Jenna ignored him and thankfully Ra'kur did too, keeping the straw in her mouth so she could drink.

"*You* dare give advice? When you did not even think she could ever waken again?" Ra'kur threw him a dark look. "Summon the senior physician! Only he should be attending her in any case."

The young doctor hurried out, the door sliding shut behind him.

Just sipping on the water was exhausting but at least she could swallow without pain now.

Ra'kur searched her face anxiously as she let go of the straw. "Can you drink more, little one?"

Jenna wet her lips. "In a minute." She glanced up at the display, at the unfamiliar equipment in the room. "We're on Hir, aren't we?"

"Yes." He gently smoothed her hair back away from her face. "I thought—I prayed to the All Mother, they said you—" He shook his head. "But you are awake and I will offer my blood to Her in thanks."

Jenna's brow creased. "What does *that* mean?"

"I will offer the Goddess my blood to thank Her."

Her frown deepened. "Not much, though, right?"

"I would give all to see you well." He gave a faint smile, his eyes shining, and inclined his head. "But this time, it will just be a little."

"You brought me to Hir."

"Yes, my Jenna."

"Even though I said I didn't want to leave Earth."

His fingers traced her cheek. "I had no choice but to bring you here. You would have died."

"Died?" She frowned. "What do you mean, 'died'?"

"You were wounded. The peacekeeper"—Ra'kur's face worked for a moment—"nearly killed you."

She stared up at him. "What are you talking about?"

"The peacekeeper shot you."

"Bill *shot* me?"

His glance went over her face. "You do not remember."

"*Bill* shot me? Sheriff Bill Riley—the man who dresses up every year as Santa for the town's Christmas party— you're telling me *Bill* shot me?"

His brow furrowed. "I do not know some of these words but the peacekeeper you call 'Bill' wounded you."

"But why the hell would he—" She broke off, looking into Ra'kur's brilliant gaze. "No," she murmured. "I don't remember. I don't remember anything about that."

He gently took her hand in his. "What is the last thing you recall?"

She considered; it was all pretty jumbled. "We were talking—arguing really—in the woods on our way to the ship so you could finish the repairs."

"You were angry. You did not want to come to my world. You left the ship to return to the shelter. I followed you. When we left tree cover we saw the peacekeeper had returned—"

"My God, he saw you, didn't he?" she whispered.

What Bill must have thought, seeing Ra'kur coming up behind her through the woods, his size, his terrifyingly inhuman face . . .

Her frightened glance went over him. "Did he shoot you too?"

"You . . . shielded me from his weapon fire." Ra'kur's eyes were haunted. "You lay on the ground, bleeding to death in the snow because you shielded *me*." He gripped her hand. "You *must* promise you will never do such a thing again!"

She was about to point out that the chances of her getting shot by an old family friend while acting as human shield had dropped significantly as soon as they left Earth's atmosphere, but then she remembered something.

The horrific sound of screams.

"Bill . . ." she whispered. "What happened to Bill?"

His glance flicked away.

"Did you hurt him, Ra'kur?" Her eyes stung with tears. "Please tell me you didn't . . . that you didn't kill him?"

His nostrils flared, his alien eyes stormy. "No," he growled. "To my shame I did not."

Her shoulders fell in relief, but—"What do you mean, to your shame?"

"I *should* have killed him." His fangs bared, wicked and sharp in this light. "I should have torn him apart."

"Bill Riley would never have meant to hurt me!" she cried, outrage giving her voice strength. "He thought I was in danger or he never would have fired." She searched his eyes. "But did—did you hurt him?"

"Yes, I hurt him," he growled. "I *wanted* to hurt him. I would have hurt him more but there was no time. I had to get you back to the ship before you—Once you were in stasis I completed the repair and brought you here."

"Do you think he . . .?"

"He reached his transport," Ra'kur said shortly. "He called for help."

Her eyes shut briefly. "Oh, thank God. But how did—"

The return of the young doctor and what she could only assume was the senior physician cut her off.

This g'hir was much older, his hair and eyebrows white, his face lined and careworn, but his carriage was proud, his blue clothes crisp.

The senior physician's glance darted over her and then moved to the display over her head. "Her baselines must be very different if she has recovered consciousness."

"It's nice to meet you too," Jenna said pointedly.

His eyes, a disconcerting vivid yellow, met hers and he came to stand at her bedside. "I am the senior physician of this facility, Doctor Elaran."

"I'm Jenna McNally."

"That is quite a namesound you have."

Somehow that didn't sound much like a compliment. And lying there, under that detached, clinical gaze, she suddenly regretted how she'd scolded Pap for the tart way he used to address his doctors.

She narrowed her eyes up at Doctor Elaran. "Okay, spit it out, already, Sawbones. How am I?"

Doctor Elaran studied the readings for a moment. She looked too as the symbols scrolled by over her head and it was really annoying that she couldn't make head or tails of them.

"I guess the question should be: how do you feel?"

"Like hell," she said honestly.

The doctor's white eyebrows rose at that. "You were grievously injured by a projectile weapon. You lost a great deal of blood and replicating it proved to be time consuming. I repaired the damage done by the projectile but your recovery from medical stasis has not gone at all as I anticipated. I would expect you do feel . . . uncomfortable."

"*You* told me she would die!" Ra'kur snarled. "You told me there was no hope!"

"Clearly I was mistaken," the doctor said dryly.

Jenna could almost hear Ra'kur gritting his teeth.

"Well?" he demanded. "Now that she lives—despite your prognosis—how is she?"

"*She* is not g'hir," the doctor reminded. "This female is the first of her species that I have ever treated. Or seen. Or *heard* of." He jerked his chin at the display. "According to these readings she should be at the All Mother's gate, but she seems to be recovering."

"*She* is also right here in the room too," Jenna snapped. "And can even be spoken to directly."

This time Doctor Elaran did look a little chagrined. "My apologies, Mata. I meant no offense."

"Mata?" she wondered, looking at Ra'kur.

"The respectful way to address a female," Ra'kur explained.

"Like 'ma'am'?" Jenna asked.

Doctor Elaran regarded her with his eerie yellow eyes. "Should I call you 'ma'am'?"

His growling attempt at the English word sounded like he was gargling the word. And, at twenty-six, she wasn't in a hurry to be addressed as 'ma'am' by anybody, thank you very much.

"No," Jenna said. "Absolutely not. By all means, use 'Mata.'"

The doctor inclined his head. "Mata. I suppose the question is—how would you describe your discomfort?"

"I'm tired," Jenna said. "Hungry. Thirsty. I ache to my bones."

"Your *bones* hurt?" Ra'kur cried.

"Warrior, you will allow me to practice the healing or I will send you outside," the doctor said sharply, then to Jenna urged: "Describe this bone pain please."

"No, that's just an expression," she said, waving her hand dismissively. "I meant my body aches. I feel sore, weak."

"Ah," the senior physician said, the tension in his shoulders easing. "The muscle aches can be explained by your time in stasis."

"You guys keep saying 'stasis.'" She looked at Ra'kur again. "Did you freeze me or something?"

"I placed you in medical suspension," he said, frowning. "It lowers the body temperature, slows the metabolism."

"So, yeah, you froze me."

"You were dying. I thank the All Mother that I reached the ship in time to place you in stasis at all." He exchanged a look with the doctors. "I do not understand why this distresses you. Is it a human taboo?"

"To be frozen like a turkey for a later, more convenient, thaw?" When she slept—even the time she'd been put under to have her appendix out—she had a sense

Willow Danes

of time passing. What really creeped her out was that this time—in stasis—she hadn't. "No, of course not. Why would it?"

"We were able to treat the considerable physical injures you suffered," Doctor Elaran said. "But you did not emerge from stasis to consciousness as you should have. All our literature pointed to stasis-induced critical failure of the brain's message center."

"But I'm not g'hir." Maybe *that's* why she had that weird time loss feeling. "So my brain is different."

"Actually, our scans have revealed the physiology of your brain to be not as different as one would expect in another species. The usual structures of the g'hir brain are present in yours." The doctor tapped his fingers against his leg for a moment. "It would stand to reason that our standard procedures to return you to consciousness should have worked."

"She may have been harmed by your ministrations," Ra'kur snapped. "Not healed."

"Again, she is my first *human*." The doctor regarded her. "But if I am to be responsible to treat you, it is best that we learn as much as possible about what is normal for your species."

Jenna shifted a little at the idea of him, of anyone, studying her.

"What matters now is to make her well," Ra'kur said sharply. "She is hungry."

The doctor pursed his lips for a moment, then gave a nod. "Yes, I think we will try some old herder's medicine. We will provide fluids and nourishment and give the body an opportunity to heal itself." The doctor glanced at his assistant. "Simple foods, to begin with. A cup of meat broth, perhaps a karlet pie later if she is up to it."

"Yes, sir," the younger g'hir murmured.

The senior physician looked back at Jenna. "I will return to check on you again in a few hours, Mata."

"He didn't say anything about this thing," Jenna complained, eying the IV in her arm after the door shut behind the two physicians.

"Does it pain you?"

"It stings a bit, yeah."

"I will tell them they must remove it," he promised.

This room had no windows. She didn't even know if it was day or night.

Oh, my God, I'm on an alien planet!

"How long have I been here, Ra'kur?"

"We arrived on Hir six days ago. You have been here, at the central medical facility in the city of Be'lyn, since we arrived."

"Six days . . ."

She couldn't even begin to imagine what was happening back home. Bill injured, herself gone, everyone and his grandmother talking about aliens—

She looked up at Ra'kur. "Are you all right?"

He gave a short, humorless laugh. "You are concerned for *me*—when you have lain bloodied and unable to wake?"

"It wasn't long ago that I was where you are now," she said quietly. "Sitting at someone's bedside, watching them hurt, knowing there was nothing else I could do. So, yeah, I want to know if you're all right."

He took her hand in his. "All that matters is that you are alive, awake, and here with me now."

"On another planet."

"You are angry, then?" he asked heavily. "You did not wish to leave your homeworld."

"What's done is done." She gave him a faint smile. "And come on. You don't think I'm busting to see your world?"

His brow creased. "You are?"

"It's an alien planet! I'm on an actual alien planet! Of *course* I want to see it." Her head felt like it weighed a ton when she lifted it, trying to see. "Is there a window out in the hall I could look out?"

Just then another g'hir, one she hadn't seen before but wearing blue scrub-like clothes like the doctors', came into her room. On the tray he carried was a bowl, steam curling from its contents and giving off a mouthwatering scent.

The man stopped when her gaze met his, his brilliant ocean blue eyes widening.

Right, I'm probably his first human too.

Jenna gave him a friendly smile and the man's mouth parted.

"Leave it and get out!" Ra'kur snarled with a gesture to the side table.

The man hurriedly did as directed, stealing little glances at her.

"That was pretty rude," Jenna said when the door slid shut behind the man.

"*He* was the rude one," Ra'kur grumbled, manipulating the bed controls to help her sit up. "To stare at you so."

Jenna fought not to groan as the new position made her light-headed. "He was just curious. I probably look really strange to your people. They've never seen a human before."

Ra'kur's nostrils flared. "It does not matter. You are a Mata. He should have more respect for you." He moved a table that extended over the bed and placed the tray in front of her.

The utensil they provided with the soup was the size of a serving spoon but Ra'kur had it in hand before she could reach for it.

She fixed him with a look. "Wait—you aren't seriously thinking you're going to *feed* me, are you?"

His gaze didn't waver. "Yes."

She studied him for a moment, considering. "*If* I let you, will you take me to a window so I can see outside?"

"When you are strong enough," he growled.

She was about to argue further but truth was, she was worn out just sitting up. Ra'kur brought the spoon to her mouth and she could almost hear Pap's voice in her head—

Best pick your battles, Birdie.

THIRTEEN

Jenna pressed her forehead against the hospital hallway window, looking longingly out at the sunlit city of Be'lyn.

"Oh, come on, Ra'kur! All I want to do is take a damned walk. I've been here cooped up in the hospital for three days now, and that doesn't count the time I was unconscious!"

"You took a walk yesterday."

She turned to face him. Now that she had been transferred out of Critical and onto a Convalescent ward she had the freedom to walk about the hospital as well as access to holographic entertainments, fascinating stuff but still— "Five minutes in the hospital's courtyard arboretum doesn't count. I want to go *outside*—into the city!"

"It is too soon," he growled. "You have only just recovered your strength."

"I'm fine and you know it. Do you have any idea what it would mean to me to get out of here for a while? Okay and maybe, you know"—she waved toward the city below, the elegant spires and enticing parklands—"*explore an alien world*?"

"I do not wish to take you among the g'hir until my clanbrothers can accompany us." He folded his arms. "It is not safe."

"What if we don't go far and just stay in populated areas?" she asked, holding the bird charm around her neck between her fingers. "We could stick to the public squares and maybe the market you told me about? Please? I really want to go."

"It would be irresponsible as your lifemate for me to take any chances with your health."

"Even Doctor Elaran okayed me for release. He said I've made 'a remarkable recovery.' I'm not even sore anymore! I'm so barely a patient now that they aren't making me wear a hospital smock," she pointed out, holding out the skirt of her new dress.

She hadn't had anything with her but the clothes on her back and those had been ruined when she was shot. She wore g'hir clothes now and in a place where a female was rare apparently they really played up the girly aspect. The lavender-colored dress she wore now was far more floaty and frilly than anything she'd worn since maybe junior prom but it and the beaded, embroidered boots Ra'kur had purchased for her were both pretty and comfortable.

"I don't even have the scar left from when I broke my arm as a kid! Credit where credit is due—g'hir medicine beats humans' hands down. And even my top-notch best-of-the-best sawbones agreed yesterday I shouldn't even *be* in the hospital. It was *your* idea to have them keep me an extra day."

"Of course he agreed with you." Ra'kur threw a dark look behind him. It was just after lunchtime—or as the g'hir called it, midmeal—and the hospital hallway was quiet now. Doctor Elaran was not likely to be back till much later for his afternoon rounds but this was one g'hir warrior who had taken a real dislike to her physician. "*He* would climb the heights of the Bruzaar Cliffs to fetch you a letari bloom if you asked."

"Hold on—you aren't seriously jealous of my doctor, are you?"

"He was content to declare there was no more to be done when you did not regain consciousness. Now he is nothing but"—Ra'kur's fangs showed—"solicitous to you."

She shrugged. "Maybe he's worried about getting sued."

Ra'kur jerked his chin at her. "What is 'sued'?"

"Well, it's when you claim someone has caused you a loss and you demand compensation."

"He should be worried." His hand brushed the weapon at his side. "We too demand payment for injuries done to us."

"Uh, where I come from it's usually *monetary* compensation. Besides . . ." Jenna put her hand on her hip. "Doctor Elaran's only interest in me is doing tests. Being that man's favorite lab rat isn't a lot of laughs, you know. There's got to be something unethical about drawing that much blood from a single subject. I feel like a damned pincushion."

Ra'kur turned toward the window. "I hate that this has been your introduction to my world—healers and their endless treatments. My clanbrothers will arrive here in a few hours to escort us to the enclosure. They have prepared a welcome for you and once we are home, you will see how beautiful—how pleasant—Hir can be."

"Which means I won't get to see the city at all before we leave," she said, and even she could hear the disappointment in her voice.

Ra'kur shifted his weight. "I suppose there will be enough peacekeepers in this area of the city to make it safe for a *short* time . . ."

"I'm ready," she said, grabbing his hand. "Let's go already!"

"You must stay close to me and we will not venture far," he warned as she pulled him down the hall toward the lift. "I do not think either of us will enjoy the attention you will get."

"Because I'm human." Her excitement at going outside suddenly dimmed a bit. The hospital staff had gotten used to her for the most part, though whenever she ventured off the floor she got some wide-eyed stares. And really, what kind of reception would Ra'kur get if she took him strolling down Page Avenue in Asheville? "Because they'll find me so alien."

He sighed. "Because they will find you so astonishing."

He wasn't kidding either. She was stared at—gawked at, really—everywhere they went. And these men didn't give hostile glares, they offered fixed, admiring looks that followed her every movement with predator-like intensity.

And it *wasn't* fun.

In every arching space she entered, every avenue, every city square, she was greeted by a ripple of stunned silence as the g'hir men paused in whatever they were doing to turn toward her, their bodies unnaturally still as they watched her with wide, luminescent eyes.

And she—with her too-round face, her brown eyes and hair—might have enjoyed creating a stir like a goddamn supermodel if it hadn't been unnerving to have so many alien males with their gazes fixed on her.

She offered the first man they encountered outside the hospital a friendly smile. The man took a step toward her, his eyes alight with interest, and Ra'kur gave a low, warning snarl, his fangs out, his hand already at the weapon at his hip.

The other g'hir hesitated and his hungry gaze flicked to her. It was a tense few seconds. Then the man took a step back.

Even with Ra'kur walking beside her and looking about as friendly as a rattler, polite smiles also proved too much of an invitation as did offering a simple nod. Jenna wasn't about to hang her head, damn it, and she strove to meet their eyes with a measure of cool respect at least.

She could count on one hand how many females she saw and each had their very own entourage of tense-looking warriors.

"Is that usual?" Jenna asked. "For a woman to be surrounded by so many men like that?"

"It was not this way before, but it has become the custom since the Scourge," Ra'kur said. "Clanbrothers now accompany a warrior and his mate to keep her safe."

"Safe from what?" The g'hir were an intimidating bunch but the capital city hardly seemed teeming with crime. She hadn't even seen any litter, for God's sake. The buildings and parks were in pristine shape, the weather mild and the air clean and sweet.

"There have been—incidents. Women who have been stolen."

Jenna blinked. "Women are kidnapped here? For ransom?"

"A female is never returned and no ransom could be high enough."

"But I thought—you said g'hir mate for life."

"Our males do."

"And the women?"

"If a male does not have the power to retrieve her, she will deem him unworthy and choose a stronger mate."

Jenna craned her neck to watch the female and her group of guards. No wonder Ra'kur was so on edge, so reluctant to take her out alone. "How often does this kind of thing happen?"

"Do not fear." His eyes were savage when they met hers. "No one will take you from me. And no enclosure would withstand the onslaught my clanbrothers will bring to get you back. Every one of them would die to protect you."

Jenna swallowed hard. "I didn't know that things were like that here." She frowned. "Would your, uh, clanbrothers do that? I mean, attack another clan for your sake?"

"Of course." He seemed surprised. "Females are our hope. You are my clan's future."

"Children." Her eyes scanned the square, the fountains, the benches, all filled with males, none younger than teenagers. "God, there are no children here either."

"There are some," he growled quietly. "Perhaps ten thousand or so on this world, on the colony worlds beyond. Perhaps we will see one today. G'hir young are very pleasing to behold."

So few, when there were millions, perhaps billions, of males here . . .

"And you want children, don't you?" Her throat tightened. Doctor Elaran had already confirmed what she'd suspected; their physiology just was too different for them to procreate. "But being with a human means you won't ever have them."

His gaze on her was soft. "I want for nothing but you, little bird." He searched her eyes and his expression grew sad. "But you, my Jenna. You wanted children."

"I've thought about it," she admitted. "Yeah, I guess I did always expect to be a mom someday."

"And for that," he said heavily, "you will need a human male."

Tears suddenly stung her eyes. He wanted kids, she did too, but they couldn't—and with children here so very precious it wasn't like there was ever going to a g'hir kid up for adoption.

She took his hand in hers. "You know what my Pap would say about now?" Jenna mimicked her grandfather's Appalachian drawl. "'Don't tell me you done foresaw *this* a comin' Birdie, and that means you can't know what life's got in store for you next. Could be best thing ever happened to you, for all you know.'"

She wasn't sure how the translator would handle the North Carolina accent but apparently it worked well enough because Ra'kur gave a faint smile.

"He was wise, your grandsire."

Jenna threw him a grin. "He'd be the first to agree with you on that."

Ra'kur tilted his head, his alien eyes brilliant in the sunlight. "I regret I did not meet him."

Jenna traced his jaw thoughtfully. "You know—if he somehow missed nailing you with the shotgun and actually could get to talking to you—I know he would have really liked you too." She tugged on his hand. "Come on, show me more of the city."

"Not much further," he warned with a look at the uniformed g'hir nearby. "There are enough peacekeepers here in the marketplace but we will not venture past this district without my clanbrothers."

Jenna suppressed a sigh. *At least I'll get to see the market.*

As they turned the corner in that direction, Jenna gasped at finding herself face to face with a large insectoid creature. Horrified, she would have fled if not for Ra'kur's hand at the small of her back.

"It is a xenari," he murmured. "They are allies of the g'hir. She will not harm you."

After a moment, her fright eased up enough to notice that the thing—the xenari—wore a shimmery dress over her dark gray exoskeleton and that her enormous multifaceted eyes seemed to be looking back at Jenna with polite curiosity.

"Good day, Mata," the xenari said.

Or rather *buzzed*.

Just like with Hironian Jenna could hear the actual sound the xenari was making but in her head she understood the words.

"Good day," Jenna stammered. *Oh, crap, he said it's a she.* "Uh, Mata."

Ra'kur inclined his head and in turn the xenari returned the gesture. After a moment of watching the enormous bug-like being warily, Jenna did the same.

Still, she couldn't keep from watching as the xenari went on her way.

"She startled you," Ra'kur said. "I should have cautioned you that there were other races who visit the capital city."

"Yeah, I, uh," Jenna began faintly, "didn't stop to think I wouldn't be the only alien in town." She glanced in the direction the xenari had gone. "I could understand her."

"The linguistic chip is standardly implanted and there are a number of other intelligent races that the g'hir have allied with."

"But none of those allies are . . . compatible?"

"Some are more pleasing to the g'hir eye than the xenari, though they are a very cultured race, but no." His gaze on her was warm. "None like you."

Most shops and stalls for clothing were of course geared toward men but there were a very few places that catered to women.

Delighted, Jenna let the smiling elderly proprietor of one such shop dab a few of the perfumes on her wrist. She couldn't detect any fragrance but the g'hir had a much better sense of smell than humans and the shopkeeper was eager for her opinion. She raised her arm to sniff to see if she noticed anything at all when she met the gaze of a richly dressed g'hir woman just arriving at the shop.

The alien female was well over six feet tall, her ridged brow far more delicate than the males fanned out around her. Her honey blond hair was thick and hung to her waist but she'd braided and decorated the front with jewels. Her radiant eyes were shown off with some kind of sparkly makeup of the same bright green shade. She wore blusher too and shimmery lipstick—no wallflowers here. The bones of her face were also finer than the males', her fitted gown showing off every curve of her rounded, feminine form.

Even in her wispy, frilly gown Jenna suddenly felt underdressed.

"Who are you?" the woman demanded.

Jenna blinked. She'd been stared at all day but no one except Ra'kur had spoken to her.

The woman looked her over. "*What* are you?"

Jenna's nostrils flared at the woman's rude tone and Ra'kur tensed beside her.

"Jenna McNally," she said coldly. "Human. I know *what* you are so I guess that just leaves *who*."

The alien woman's lips parted at having been addressed in kind.

I guess when you're a gorgeous female g'hir, you get used to a lot of people talking sweet to you.

Jenna folded her arms. "You have a name, don't you? Or did you leave it back home 'long with your manners?"

The woman's eyes widened and then she gave a sudden, delighted laugh, her delicate fangs flashing in the sunlight.

"My apologies, Mata," she said, her eyes crinkled with humor. "Indeed, I was impolite. I am Si'hala, of the Yir clan enclosure." She indicated the warrior at her side. "My mate, Lihr."

Jenna offered Lihr a nod then felt her cheeks heat when she realized she had to introduce Ra'kur. She could hardly call him her boyfriend and "mate" didn't sound right either. They hadn't even talked about what was going to happen next. "This is Ra'kur."

"Of the Erah enclosure," he supplied.

"I have heard of your clan," Lihr growled, his spring green eyes respectful. "The Erah lands are in the Araki territory."

Ra'kur inclined his head. "Yes. In the Zun Mountains."

"Good hunting there?" Lihr asked.

Si'hala looked round at him. "*Hunting?*"

"I am making good acquaintance with an honored warrior, Si'hala," Lihr said with a narrowed glance.

"Very good hunting," Ra'kur said, and even Jenna could tell he was trying to smooth things over.

"There is a new alien female standing right in front of us and you are talking about *hunting?*" She looked at Jenna and gave a headshake. "Males! Are they different on your world, human?"

Jenna threw Ra'kur an impish look. "Not really. But," Jenna continued, turning back to Si'hala, "we really wouldn't want them to be, would we?"

The g'hir woman sent a fond glance at her mate and her pretty fangs flashed again. "No, I suppose we wouldn't."

Si'hala jerked her chin toward Jenna but addressed the shopkeeper. "Are those the new scents from the Ki territory?"

The elderly g'hir stepped forward quickly. "Yes, Mata."

Jenna held up her arm to sniff again. She could detect a very faint flowery scent from one of the samples he'd placed on her arm; it smelled a little like jasmine.

"I like the middle one." Jenna held her wrist out to the g'hir woman. "What do you think?"

It was the kind of thing she'd do out shopping with a girlfriend but the woman blinked and the warriors with her looked equally surprised. G'hir had different mannerisms, a different culture; hell, they were a different *species* so maybe she'd just made a social blunder.

Jenna was about to drop her arm and apologize when Si'hala stepped forward and sniffed.

"Very nice." She met Jenna's eye. "It suits you, Mata."

"You can call me Jenna."

The g'hir female straightened and regarded her for a moment then inclined her head. "Jenna."

Jenna felt like she was missing something here but she couldn't ask Ra'kur right now. She looked at the shopkeeper. "I guess I'll take it then." Oh, crap, she didn't have any money. She looked at Ra'kur. "Uh, okay?"

"Purchase whatever you please," Ra'kur said, his bright eyes warm. "The Erah clan has waited long to welcome a new Mata."

"Right," Jenna managed, shifting her weight.

"I believe," Si'hala put in, "that a yellow silk gown would suit you very well too." The g'hir woman looked at the shopkeeper. "Bring us—No, never mind." She caught hold of Jenna's arm. "We will come inside to look." She gave an imperious look at the men with her. "Wait here."

To Jenna's surprise not only did they not protest, Ra'kur didn't either.

Probably confident nothing will happen to us inside the shop.

"Bring us that one," Si'hala said, pointing. "The yellow silk with the ribbon embroidery." The g'hir female eyed her as the elderly shopkeeper hurried to fetch the dress. "How long have you been on Hir?"

"Only a few days. Actually I was injured before Ra'kur brought me here," she supplied before Si'hala could ask. "This is my first time out of the hospital."

The g'hir woman tilted her head. "Where is your world?"

"I don't know actually," Jenna admitted. "Ra'kur says it's very far from Hir, that it takes an enormous amount of power to get here."

"Then you are the only human here?"

Jenna frowned. She wasn't sure where Si'hala was going with all these questions. "As far as I know."

Si'hala looked her over, her green glowing glance measuring. "Are there more of your kind coming, Jenna? Females?"

"Not that I know of," Jenna said warily. "Would that be a problem?"

Si'hala lifted an eyebrow. "No, the g'hir need more females and certainly new fashions—if your people care about such things. Ours seem to keep coming up with the same things year after year."

Jenna had a sudden image of Si'hala in the front row for Paris' fashion week and she smiled. "Oh, well in that case, I think our people would have a lot to offer yours."

"It is obvious," Si'hala gave a nod at her clothes, "that your mate chose your dress."

Jenna looked down at herself. "Something wrong with it?"

"It is a winter color." The g'hir female sniffed. "*No one* is wearing it now." She waved the shopkeeper over and took the yellow gown from him to hold it in front of Jenna. "Shades of yellows and greens are for spring, not purple. And you are not wearing any jewels. We will fix that as well." Si'hala snapped her fingers at the shopkeeper and jerked her chin toward another dress, a bright lemon yellow. "Bring us that one as well."

"So you're giving me a fashion makeover?" Jenna asked, not sure whether to be flattered or annoyed by the g'hir woman's efforts.

"Make*over*." Si'hala smiled. "Yes, I will make*over* until you look good." The g'hir woman held the lemon-colored gown in front of her and frowned thoughtfully. "This is not terrible. Perhaps once we have done something with your hair so it does not simply *hang* there it will be flattering."

"Hey, thanks," Jenna said, deciding to go with annoyed after all. "You know—since I can only pick between the two or face fashion oblivion—I actually like green better than yellow."

"Do not be ridiculous," Si'hala said with an airy wave. "*I* am wearing green. We cannot both leave the shop wearing the same color."

"Sorry," Jenna muttered as the g'hir woman urged her toward the fitting room. "Don't know what I was thinking."

An hour, and Jenna didn't want to think how much g'hir currency, later, Si'hala deemed her outfitted as a Mata should be. The shopkeeper promised to have the other dresses—Si'hala allowed her to purchase a few of the green ones for later wear—sent straight away to the Erah enclosure. In truth, Jenna suspected that the g'hir woman was showing her a real kindness by doing all this. The men seemed to be getting along well outside and Ra'kur's eyes lit up when he saw her.

She ducked her head shyly at his appreciative look. "I'm sorry we took so long in there."

He smiled. "I am pleased you have enjoyed your time but we should return to the hospital. My clanbrothers have signaled. They will arrive there shortly." He looked at Lihr and Si'hala. "Perhaps the Yir clan will consider a visit. My mate is new to this world and the Erah have few females in our number. I am sure she would welcome more of your companionship, Mata."

Si'hala smiled. "I did enjoy the makeover, Jenna."

"I did too," Jenna said. "Thank you."

"I am very happy to have met you," Si'hala said warmly. "I look forward to our next meeting."

"You think she meant that?" Jenna asked, with a final wave at the Yir before they turned the corner and vanished from sight.

"I am certain she did."

"So I made my first alien girlfriend?"

"I would say so, my Jenna. But come." He caught her hand in his, smiling down at her. "My clanbrothers await us now."

When Ra'kur and Jenna arrived at the hospital's windy landing platform she saw that five of his clanbrothers waited near the transport vessel to escort them to the Erah territory. Their eyes were sharp and she didn't miss how their hands hovered over their weapons.

Fortunately not many others besides their party occupied the elevated platform right now. As she and Ra'kur approached the clanbrothers their gazes turned to her with the same surprised looks she'd garnered in the city and she was already feeling overwhelmed. Dressed much as Ra'kur was in dark brown leather, their hair color ran from his black to a light chocolate brown. With their eyes varying brilliant shades of blue these men showed clear resemblance to him, especially one.

"Ke'lar!" Ra'kur said, warmly embracing the man.

The man clapped him on the back, smiling. "It has been too long, brother."

Ke'lar was a bit shorter than Ra'kur—which still made him pretty darn tall in Jenna's eyes. His face was full of good humor as he turned to her, his blue eyes as bright as his brother's. "You did not exaggerate. Your mate is very beautiful."

Jenna's face warmed. "Uh, thanks."

"And your way of speaking is very soothing to the ear." Ke'lar tilted his head. "Are there any others like you, Mata?"

"You mean human women?" Jenna asked, surprised. "Of course. Lots of them."

Ke'lar's gaze darted to his brother. "Give me the location of this world." He glanced at the other men who looked just as interested. "We will depart as soon as you are safe within the enclosure."

"Oh, hold on!" Jenna cried. "You can't just show up on my planet and start grabbing women! You shouldn't be in an all-fire rush anyway. You might get mates but Dr. Elaran is certain g'hir and humans can't have children."

"But Mata," Ke'lar began, "if there is even a possibility that there are females to whom we can be lifemated—"

"This is something to be discussed within the security of the enclosure," Ra'kur interrupted sharply, sending a meaningful glance toward other men nearby, not of their clan, coming and going from their own transports on the landing platform.

"Of course," Ke'lar murmured, crestfallen, and Jenna felt sorry for him. It wasn't like she wanted these guys to spend their lives alone but the whole idea of them heading for Earth unnerved her. "The whole clan has come to welcome our new Mata."

The men parted to allow them entrance to the transport vessel.

"The whole clan?" Jenna asked Ra'kur as they stepped onboard. "How many people are we talking about here?"

He shrugged. "A few hundred."

"A few *hundred*?" she echoed as they took their seats. "To meet me? God, *why*?"

He gave her a surprised look. "You are very important, Jenna. You are the first female to join our clan in years." His glance went over her face. "You are nervous? You should not be."

"Oh, heck, no," she said, fingering the bird charm around her neck as the other clanbrothers stepped aboard and the transport door shut to prepare for liftoff. "Not nervous at all."

Fourteen

Dismayed, Jenna looked out over the rows and rows of g'hir warriors assembled for her arrival and swallowed hard.

"Come." Ra'kur took her hand to lead her forward. "They are eager to welcome you home."

"Home," she murmured. "Right."

Standing in front of a crowd or even having to give a speech in class in college rattled her but having Ra'kur's strong warm hand in hers sure made it easier.

She walked down the ramp of the transport ship that had brought them from Be'lyn City, nervous enough that she was worried about tripping over her own feet. They had actually entered Erah territory an hour ago and Jenna watched wide-eyed as miles upon miles of woodlands blurred by beneath their transport.

And she'd been bragging on her five hundred acres.

The Erah enclosure itself was the size of a town built up around a central square. Ra'kur explained that the fountain here was fed by the same springs that provided water to the residents of the enclosure. The buildings themselves were reddish in color and strongly resembled adobe houses even though the weather here was more like the northeast than the southwest. It was warm today, spring for this region, and the foliage was verdant and lush.

The rows of warriors stood silently as Ra'kur led her forward, Ke'lar following them down the ramp, the g'hirs' stance inhumanly, unnaturally still as they watched.

An older man, his long hair salt and pepper but his back straight and proud, came forward to meet them. A younger g'hir, moving with the awkward gawkiness of a teenager, came too.

The older man embraced Ra'kur and his growl trembled a little with emotion. "It has been so long since you went from us, my son, that I feared you dead."

Ra'kur hugged him back. "I am glad to be home, Father." He drew back to look at Jenna with shining eyes. "And to have brought a mate home with me." He took her hand in his again. "Jenna, this is my sire, Rotin. Father"— he gave her a warm, proud look—"this is my Jenna."

In his face were deep creases of pain and grief but Rotin's electric blue eyes rested on her kindly. "You are most welcome to the Erah clan, Jenna, and to our enclosure."

"Thank you. It's beautiful," Jenna said honestly.

"Jenna has never left her own world. She has never seen a person who is not human."

"Is *that* what you are?" the younger man blurted. "Human?"

"Tarsh!" Rotin scolded; the boy's face reddened and he dropped his gaze, mumbling an apology.

Ra'kur blinked. "This is Tarsh? You have grown so I did not recognize you!"

"You have been gone for six years," Tarsh said, his growl sulky. "Of course I have grown."

"Our younger brother, Tarsh," Ke'lar said to Jenna. "His manners are usually better."

"I'm pleased to meet you," Jenna said. "And yeah, I'm a human."

Tarsh jerked his chin toward her, his incandescent eyes a paler blue than his brothers'. "Are there a lot of humans?"

She gave a nod. "Yup. Billions."

"*Billions?*" Ke'lar exclaimed. "How many are female?"

Jenna could have bitten her tongue and Ra'kur, at least, noticed her discomfiture.

"I think we should complete Jenna's welcome to the clan," he said with a warning look at Ke'lar. "Before we badger her with questions about her world."

"Of course," Rotin agreed. "We have a celebration prepared in your honor." He extended his hand to indicate the large central building of the enclosure. "Please, Mata, we are honored to welcome you home."

She wasn't sure if it would be more accurate to call the place a mansion or a palace but the house Ra'kur's family called home was huge.

"Wow," she murmured, getting her first look at the inside, at the soaring spaces and decorative work, as they followed Ra'kur's father inside. With his height Ra'kur had to duck through every door in her cabin but he sure wouldn't have to duck in here. The space was also filled with alien flowers and bright streamers, no doubt done for her benefit.

Ra'kur stayed protectively at her side, her hand tucked into his. His brothers walked behind them and a glance back showed that the rest of the g'hir warriors were following them inside.

"Our clan has resided in this enclosure for centuries," Ra'kur said with a proud look at the space. "This center hall is nearly a thousand years old."

"Your family has lived here for a thousand years?" Jenna managed. "It's beautiful."

"But ill-matched," Ra'kur put in with a laugh. "The rest of the buildings—and a great deal of this one—are newer. Every generation builds, remodels, expands the enclosure—"

"But since the Scourge," Rotin said, a shadow passing over his face, "there has been no need to expand the living quarters, and many of them stand empty."

"Father," Ke'lar pleaded. "Not now. Please."

"You are right, of course." Rotin gave her a faint smile. "I apologize. My sons will tell you my mood sometimes turns dark on the brightest of days. As today is, Mata." He nodded toward huge arched doors that had been thrown open to a hall also cheerfully decorated. "The Erah Matas are eager to make your acquaintance."

Inside the hall waited a handful of female g'hir, their eyes curious on her. Two were elderly, one appeared to be a teenager, and one, accompanied by two little girls, was about her own age.

The children were adorable, with rounded, soft faces and big eyes that stared up at her. The elder girl looked to be about six, her sister a few years younger, and they hung back shyly as they were introduced. Even the girls' fangs were cute and these little ones were obviously the treasures of the enclosure. Their hair, golden in color like their mother's, was braided, curled, and beribboned. Their dresses, miniature versions of ladies' gowns, were in soft greens that emphasized their youth and pink cheeks.

Rotin introduced each of the women in turn. They each offered words of welcome but Yalar, mother of the two girls, was a bit cool and kept her children close at her side.

Jenna's eyes were drawn to the scores of warriors filling the dining hall.

"Is that all of them?" she asked Ra'kur quietly after introductions were made and the g'hir started moving around the room, making their way to their seats. "All of the women in your clan?"

He glanced at the female with the two young girls as the woman's mate proudly escorted his family to their seats. "I have not met Yalar before; she came to the enclosure after I left. With her children, and you, we have many more females than before."

"With me that makes seven," she murmured.

He gave her a smile. "The All Mother has blessed us."

Jenna swallowed hard. Ra'kur was right; their race was dying. If—and it was a big damn if—they managed to survive it would take centuries for them to rebuild their species.

No wonder Ke'lar and the other clanbrothers were ready to take off immediately for Earth. They had about zero chance of ever having a mate here.

Dozens of pairs of alien eyes watched her every move. Some of the males stole glances and some showed open hunger, obvious envy for their clanbrother.

She was seated at the head table between Rotin and Ra'kur and flanked by Rotin's other sons. Her eyes widened at the feast they set before her. She was no judge of their cuisine, of course, but just the variety and skill of presentation of the dishes placed on the table bespoke of a great deal of care and attention.

"You shouldn't have gone to so much trouble," she demurred as they filled her plate with meats and different side dishes, some featuring very strange-looking vegetables.

"Why not?" Tarsh demanded. "Are you not staying?"

"Of course she is staying!" Ke'lar said impatiently. "She is your clansister now. This is her home."

Jenna tried to hide her dismay but Ra'kur caught her expression and his brow furrowed a little.

"That's just something people say where I come from," she explained to Tarsh, lifting her two-pronged fork. The utensil felt a bit too big in her hand and she felt self-conscious trying to spear a piece of meat. "A way of saying thank you for all that you've done."

"It is our joy to welcome you here, Mata," Rotin said. "As it is to have Ra'kur home."

"At last," Ke'lar said with a fond look at his brother, then to Jenna: "He was gone a very long time."

"I searched far for my Jenna," Ra'kur said with a warm look at her. "Many star systems, many worlds."

"You must tell us all about your world, Mata," Ke'lar said.

It sounded like polite conversation, asking someone about where they're from, the kind of thing you'd ask a new acquaintance, but Jenna knew that's not what this was about.

And unless she was prepared to be rude, there wasn't much way around it.

"I don't know what to say." She was uncomfortable telling them anything about Earth. "I've never been anywhere else."

"Their space travel is limited to their own star system," Ra'kur said.

"A primitive culture then," Ke'lar murmured. "With limited weaponry?"

"But a whole lotta fight," Jenna said sharply.

There was an awkward pause.

"You must try this cali fruit custard," Rotin said, already scooping some onto her plate, and for just a moment, despite the ridges on his forehead and alien eyes, he reminded her of Pap.

There's nobody to put flowers on Pap's grave. All our photos, the pocket watch Pap's granddaddy left him, it's all there in the cabin still. What will happen to all of it now?

Rotin was still waiting for her to try the custard and Jenna lifted her spoon.

"It's wonderful," she murmured, tasting it. The custard had a light sweetness to it and reminded her a bit of the flavor of kiwis.

"It is made from cali fruit grown within our own enclosure."

"How big is the Erah enclosure?" she asked, determined to keep the topic of conversation *off* Earth.

"We have fifteen hundred hectares," Rotin said. "But our clan numbers only six hundred now."

And just seven of them females.

"Is that a lot of land for an enclosure?" she asked.

Rotin shrugged, but alien or not she could read the pride of landowner in his face. "Larger than most, not as large as some."

"I look forward to showing it to you," Ra'kur said. "Although I expect there have been many changes during my absence." He sent her a smile. "We could ride the land tomorrow. We have transports but we still ride beasts called multari, like our ancestors did. They rode similar beasts in the images."

"Images?" Jenna wondered.

"The images," he reminded. "The tale of Charles and his lifemate Nell."

"Oh, right," she said with a laugh. "I forgot about that movie. The animals they rode in *The Gentleman Rogue* are called horses."

"The multari are not so different from your worlds' horses."

"Well, I can ride a horse," she said. "I guess we'll find out how well I handle a multari."

Ra'kur was skillful at keeping the topic of conversation to Hir and matters important to the Erah clan for the rest of the meal.

More sweets were served at the conclusion of the feast and Jenna noticed they were soft-textured selections—custards and stewed fruits, no cakes or pies like back home. As she sampled the various offerings, Yalar and her daughters sang for the group. The translated words were lovely but if Jenna concentrated only on what her ears were getting it just sounded like a bunch of snarls and growls.

She also found out the hard way that the g'hir didn't applaud at the end of a performance. Her face hot before the crowd's startled eyes, she was forced into a quick, embarrassed explanation of that human custom.

Light was fading from the sky. Jenna was stiff from sitting by the feast's end and pretty worn out by the time dinner ended. Shy now in the wake of her clapping blunder, she thanked Rotin for their hospitality as people were getting to their feet.

"There is no need to thank us," Rotin said. "You are part of our clan, it has been our honor to welcome you home."

"This hand hitting is an interesting practice," Ke'lar said quickly. "I would like to know more about human customs."

"I am sure there will be ample opportunity in the coming days, brother," Ra'kur said, taking her hand. "But it has been a long day and my mate is fatigued. I must take her to our quarters."

Rotin gave a kindly nod but Ke'lar looked disappointed.

"He's not going to let this go, is he?" Jenna murmured with a look back at the dispirited young warrior as Ra'kur led her into the hallway.

"I cannot fault him for it," Ra'kur said ruefully. "He wishes only for what I have. For a female to pledge himself to, to build a life with."

Jenna suddenly found it hard to meet his eyes.

"If he badgers you about your world, you must tell him he is just being lazy," Ra'kur said, his tone lighter as they ascended the wide staircase to the clanhall's second level. "You did notice that he did not volunteer to spend years spaceward in search?"

She laughed. "You know, you're right. Seems kinda unfair, now that you mention it. Did they make it tough on you before you left? When you decided to go out looking?"

"You mean did any of my clan try to dissuade me from venturing out into space to search for a lifemate? Call me a fool and a madman?" He gave a grin. "Yes, little bird, every last one of them."

"You have a lot of courage," she said. "To go against the grain."

"No," he said softly, stopping. "I knew in my heart, even as a boy, that someday I would find you and bring you home."

He nodded at the open door ahead to indicate she should precede him inside.

The living space was huge, larger than the whole of Pap's cabin had been. The ceilings were high, white and domed, the walls a warm brown, the floor beneath a mosaic of blue and green glass tiles that glittered in the soft lighting as she explored. Furniture, suited to the larger g'hir bodies and upholstered in soft earth-toned fabrics, was placed into comfortable conversation areas around the space.

There were bedrooms on either side of the central living area. The largest was dominated by a huge carved wooden bed and more of that plush furniture, the smaller ones clearly meant for children. There were two private bathrooms. The one off the master bedroom was done in ocean blue and teal tiles and featured a sunken bath as deep and wide as a hot tub. The apartment had a small kitchen—though none of the equipment there looked familiar—and a balcony that ran the length of the entire outer wall.

"Wow," she breathed, her eyes wide. "*These* are your quarters?"

He laughed. "These are *our* quarters. An unmated warrior, even a son of the clanfather, does not warrant living space such as this."

"So this is for my benefit." She tucked her hair behind her ear. "They're going to a lot of trouble for me."

"They want you to be happy in your new home," he growled softly. "As do I."

She stepped out onto the balcony to look out over the land.

"Clanfather . . ." She looked up at him as the realization hit. "Ra'kur, are you in line to be the clan's leader?"

"I am the eldest," he agreed. "Someday I will be clanfather and you will take your place beside me to lead. It has been many years since the Erah had a clanmother."

Jenna wet her lips. "I get that being a clanmother must be a big deal, a huge honor, but everything here is so different. I feel so"—she gave a short laugh—"*alien*. I'm not sure where my place is anymore. I mean to me it's like one minute I had two feet square on my own land and the next I woke up on another planet. Right now, I feel really . . . lost."

Hir's moons shone cool light over the forests of the Erah enclosure's territory below and she leaned against the balcony wall.

"And I just—I don't know what I'd do here," she said finally, a lump forming in her throat, knowing those smaller bedrooms would never be used.

"You can do anything, my Jenna. Females filled every profession and level of influence before the Scourge. They have even more freedom to choose now. Half the ruling council of Hir is female and I would deny you nothing that brought you joy." He tilted his head. "What were you going to do on Earth?"

"Well . . . I have a degree in business but I used to have a bakery in Asheville called The Sweet Tooth. It was doing pretty well too. I was actually thinking about opening another one in Charlotte. But when Pap got sick I couldn't keep up with everything and take care of him proper like I ought; I sure as hell wasn't gonna to hire a stranger to tend him so I closed the doors. That broke him up the worst, you know, feeling that him getting sick cost me my business. We talked about it before he went." She swallowed hard at the memory, looking out at the moonlit land of this other world. "He wanted me to reopen, sell the land he left me and use all that money to take The Sweet national, to get back all I lost and more besides."

Ra'kur wrapped his arms around her waist, his body warm against her back. "I recall the confections you made for me. The brownies. The hummingbird cake. The cooks."

"Cookies," she corrected, smiling. "They're called cookies."

"You could do that here, if you like. The clan will purchase property for you in Be'lyn City, or another city, if you prefer."

"Expand my bakery brand to an alien planet?" she asked as she turned toward him. "Somehow that didn't make it onto my original business plan."

"The g'hir will enjoy the confections," he promised. "You will be very successful."

"Yeah, there's the little matter of reaching my suppliers," she said, thinking of how different the foods were here, how she hadn't even recognized the kitchen equipment in the galley of his ship or here in the apartment. "I don't have the ingredients to make the things I used to have at The Sweet Tooth."

"Could you not then make confections from things we have here?" he asked, taking her hands in his. "But made your way?"

"Maybe," she allowed. "But everything's back there, on Earth. All my recipes and cookbooks. And everything of Pap's too, and things *his* folks left him. Photos of me and him, of my parents and Becca, too." She swallowed hard. "Things are so different here. There's three moons over my head, for god's sake! I'd have to relearn how to cook, figure out how to bake things I did before or invent new ways of doing it."

"If you want to do this, if it will make you happy," he said, touching his forehead to hers, "then you will do it."

In fact she had the feeling that the Erah clan—Ra'kur really—would keep any business she opened going indefinitely, even if she was a huge flop, just to keep her happy.

He shouldn't have to do that, try so hard to make a life for her here. That was her responsibility.

And that was the real problem. She couldn't be half here and half on Earth, just halfheartedly committed to Ra'kur. It wasn't fair to either one of them.

"What if"—she wet her lips—"what if I wanted to go home? Go back to my own world?"

He went very still. "Do you?"

"I don't know," she said honestly. "I don't know what I want yet." She put her hands on his chest. "But . . . but if I choose Earth?"

His face was grave. "I cannot live with you there, my Jenna."

She dropped her gaze. "I know," she said quietly.

Gently he tilted her face up to look into her eyes.

"Nothing means more to me than your happiness, little bird," he said hoarsely. "If you choose Earth . . . I vow to you, I will take you back."

"Okay." Jenna let her breath out. "Okay."

"You have not seen much of my world. Hardly anything but healers and the hospital. Please," he said, his voice strained, "do not make your choice yet. Let me show you what my world—what I—can offer you."

FIFTEEN

Jenna had ridden her share of horses but that didn't mean she was sure about handling a multari.

First off, the damned thing was the size of a Clydesdale. Intimidating enough, but it also had disconcerting glowing yellow eyes that were looking right back at her now with about as much confidence in her ability to ride it as she was feeling.

Ra'kur, too, was regarding her with concern. "Jenna?"

"It looks like one of those creatures from the ancient Greek myths," she said. "You know, the ones that have a homing beacon set on Hades?"

"This one is the most mild-tempered beast," Ke'lar assured, patting the thing's neck affectionately. "Her mouth is tender and she is obedient." He gave a slight smile. "I would not endanger my brother's mate—and risk my only hope to learn the location of your world."

Jenna reached a cautious hand toward the multari to stroke the warm buff-colored hair of the creature's long nose. The multari gave a snort, her yellow eyes rolling a bit, her hooves shifting restlessly.

Ra'kur hadn't mounted yet, confidently holding the reins of his own fearsome-looking dun-colored multari. "We do not have to ride, little bird. We can take ground transport instead."

Considering how thickly forested the enclosure was, she already knew that the view from the road of a ground transport would be mainly trees blurring by. They would be better off walking.

"No," she said, forcing confidence into her voice simply because the multari was listening. "I'm going to ride."

"Let me help you," Ra'kur said, ready to hand the reins of his animal to Ke'lar.

"Nope," she said. She was wearing dark green trousers, jacket, and boots not so different from Ra'kur's usual clothes for their outing. The leather of her clothing was very soft and supple, the cut quite suitable to a female figure. "I can do this on my own."

Just like with a horse, she went to the left side and put her foot into the stirrup. She was lucky she was tall or she would have needed a mounting block to even get on the thing. Even with her height she had to bounce a bit to get high enough to use the muscles of her thigh to swing over.

But she managed to get into the saddle by herself.

Despite her best intentions her fingers were trembling a bit as she took the reins from Ke'lar. The multari shifted, all anxiety and restless muscles underneath her as Ke'lar adjusted the stirrup length to suit her better. She swallowed hard at how far away the ground was as he stepped back. She wouldn't want to take a fall from this height and she felt a little dizzy from imagining it.

Ra'kur swung up into the saddle easily. "We will go slowly," he promised. He turned his multari and nudged it a bit with his heels to get it going. "There is a place I especially wish to show you, but it is not far."

Too nervous to answer, Jenna gave a quick nod, her heart giving a jump as the multari started at a walk.

As they left the buildings and gardens of the enclosure and ventured into the surrounding forest Jenna tried to shift her focus from the huge, powerful beast she was riding to the alien world around her.

Ra'kur was right, it wasn't so very different from Earth in that plants were green, the sky was blue; she could almost believe she was somewhere back home enjoying a beautiful spring day bathed in sunshine. Except of course Hir had two suns, one much paler and farther from the planet than the other, making that golden light. The flowers that carpeted the open fields were glorious pinks, purples, and blues and a group of tangerine-colored birds hopped nearby pecking at the ground.

"Does it snow here?" she asked.

"Yes," Ra'kur said with a smile. "Traditionally the clan gathers at first snowfall, and other than to tend the beasts, the g'hir customarily stay within the enclosure until the weather warms. Winter is a time of storytelling, crafts, and marriages." His smile turned rueful. "But marriages are rare now."

"So . . . there's a difference between lifemating and marriage?"

"Lifemating is first and private," he said with a wolfish grin. "Marriage comes after and is public. Marriages are done at midwinter only. It used to be that a female would travel to the enclosure for the first snow and remain with her chosen until midwinter. If they had lifemated, there would be a marriage. If not," he shrugged, "she would return to her clan or depart for another enclosure."

"I guess that's kind of like dating," Jenna offered. "Getting to know a prospective mate."

"Our date was very enjoyable. I am glad I could honor your customs."

She blinked. "Our date? When did we have a date?"

"Dinner." He tilted his head. "A movie. Fucking."

He was in absolute earnest and Jenna had to bite the inside of her cheek not to laugh. "Yeah, I liked it too."

'Course if memory serves we didn't actually make it all the way through the movie. . .

"So, that's nice," she said, "that everyone gathers to spend the winter together."

"Our kind has always done so. Our archeological records show even our ancestors did. In spring we venture out to gather and hunt. That was the hardest time for me— winter," he said. "When I knew the others were gathering and I would not be with them."

"Because you were in space."

"I do not regret it." His eyes had a funny look to them when they met hers. "No matter what comes."

"When you were out searching did you uh . . . find any other females, besides me?"

"I found females who were attractive," he said reluctantly. "But none that were compatible." His face flushed a bit. "None that I could lifemate to."

But he tried.

"You know what?" she muttered, jamming her heels sharply into the multari's sides. "Let's try riding faster."

She got her multari up to what felt like a trot and Ra'kur matched her pace. The forest became denser so that they were forced to ride singly; then suddenly they were out from the treeline and Jenna drew her breath deeply in appreciation. The land sloped downward slightly to a clear lake and in the distance the majestic snow-capped mountains ringed the valley.

He reined in and threw her a smile. "What do you think, little bird?"

"You were right; your world is beautiful." She gave a laugh. "You know, this is the perfect spot for a picnic."

"What is that?"

"A meal, eaten outside," she said. "Usually you bring a blanket and spread it out, then just eat and lie around and be lazy."

He gave a nod, his eyes shining. "We will do so on our next ride."

She looked at the lake. "Can we swim in it?"

His smile widened. "If you like."

"Why do I suddenly have the feeling that your people don't have swimsuits?" She had her answer from the quizzical look he gave her. "Usually my people wear something specially designed for swimming. The fabric is tight and stretchy and dries fast. Going swimming with nothing on is called 'skinny dipping.'"

"Ah," he said. "That is what g'hir do then—skinny dipping. I did bring emergency rations but no blanket and I think you will find the food at the enclosure more palatable. We should ride back now if we are to make it in time for midmeal."

"Because I ride so slowly?" she asked with a glance at the sky. "How fast can the multari run, anyway?"

"Fast," he said, turning his mount back toward the enclosure. "I could not catch one on foot."

"That's pretty fast," she said, tightening her grip on the reins.

It was a lovely ride and thanks to Jenna's greater confidence they made it back with an hour to spare.

"There is time enough to take a walk in the orchards before midmeal," he said with a nod in that direction after they'd handed off the reins to one of the multari's tenders. "If you like."

"That sounds great."

But as they came around the stable Ra'kur stopped short. Jenna too noticed the transport resting on the earthen tiles of the sunny courtyard, an official-looking symbol emblazoned on its side.

"I guess you have a visitor?"

"Yes," Ra'kur growled, already changing direction to enter the main house. "An unwelcome one."

SIXTEEN

Ke'lar was pacing in the soaring entrance hall when she and Ra'kur arrived and two uniformed g'hir stood at attention outside the dining room. Their uniforms didn't mean anything to Jenna but by the way Ra'kur glowered they obviously did to him. Ke'lar and Ra'kur exchanged a look and his brother sent a tense glance at the dining hall's archway.

Ra'kur's jaw hardened. Jenna had to hurry to keep up with his long strides as he headed that way.

Inside the hall Rotin was seated at the long gleaming wood table with another older man, one dressed smartly in tunic and pants, a fancy-looking sash over his shoulder to cross his chest. There were more uniformed guards here too, standing at attention at the far end of the hall, and it was easy to guess they belonged to this man.

She barely knew her new father-in-law but she could tell right off he wasn't happy about having this guy here either.

The sashed g'hir man stood and turned as soon as she and Ra'kur entered, and he stared unabashedly at her.

"They told me," he said, his eyes fixed on her. "They told me, but I did not believe . . ."

"Hello," she said uneasily when he trailed off. "I'm Jenna."

The man's mouth curved into a smile and he reminded her a lot of the guy in Hendersonville who'd sold her that truck right out of college. Pap called it death on wheels and hollered holy hell till they took it back and he issued her a refund.

"Greetings, Mata, I am—"

"What are you doing here, Mirak?" Ra'kur demanded.

"I have come to welcome your mate to Hir, of course." He offered Jenna a short bow. "I am Mirak of the Betari enclosure. I am also a member of the Hir's ruling council."

"Do males make a habit of visiting the Matas of rival clans now?" Ra'kur folded his arms. "Things must have changed a great deal in my absence."

"None of the enclosures can afford to be rivals these days," Mirak said sharply. "Our people are a generation from virtual extinction."

"I know why you are here, Mirak," Ra'kur snarled.

"He is concerned that I have come to steal you away," Mirak said to Jenna with a shrug that revealed some bitterness. "But my few guards are no match for an enclosure full of enraged Erah clanbrothers. I am long past my prime and my own mate, Esiri, long dead. I certainly do not come here to lure you away with *my* charms."

"You have a son," Ra'kur pointed out. "And many clanbrothers, do you not? And my mate is very beautiful."

"No offense to you, Mata, but my Esiri was far more so—at least in my eyes." He cleared his throat. "In any case, no, I have not come to make some foolhardy attempt at stealing your mate. I have come to warn you."

Ra'kur and Rotin exchanged a glance.

"*You* wish to warn me?" Ra'kur scoffed. "Warn me about what?"

"That while I have no interest in tearing this lovely female from you," he said with a nod at Jenna, "others do."

Ra'kur's gaze narrowed. "I already know this. You have wasted my time—and your own—in coming here to tell me so."

"Others"—Mirak's face was grave—"on the ruling council."

Ra'kur blinked and his fangs flashed. "They have no right!"

Mirak inclined his head a little. "Agreed."

"Hold on a damned minute!" Jenna broke in. "What the hell are you two talking about?"

Mirak met her gaze. "After what I can imagine was a long and exhaustive search, a son of the Erah clan has returned with a mate from a people not before seen. Not just a compatible mate but a very attractive and plainly intelligent one. Word reached the ruling council of you, Mata, before you left the surgical bay." Mirak folded his hands in front of him. "My esteemed colleagues have been gathering intelligence on you ever since and, sad but true, many of the hospital staff have cooperated in this fact-finding."

"Okay," Jenna gritted out. "They know my blood type. Hurrah for them. What do they want?"

"You. Or more accurately"—Mirak raised his eyebrows—"more like you."

Jenna felt herself blanch. "An invasion. You're talking about going to Earth and taking women by force."

Mirak gave a nod. "We have allied with other species but since none have been compatible candidates, intermating has never been an issue before. Now it has suddenly become a vital—no, a crucial—problem to be addressed."

Jenna wet her lips. "But Ra'kur and I can't—"

"The ruling council has already been apprised that breeding with your kind will not be possible," Mirak interrupted. "Some are opposed to bringing human females here in any great number even without the chance of offspring. But when it becomes public knowledge that our males have hope of a lifemate of their own . . ." A shadow passed over Mirak's face. "It did occur to one of the ruling council—whom I will not name now—that human children, along with a large-scale importation of females, might too prove to be a boon to our society."

"That's despicable," she managed. "That's appalling."

"I would rather not see it come to that," Mirak said, straightening. "I would not have the g'hir people descend into the despicable echelon of *slavers*. And so I have come to propose an alliance between my clan and yours, Ra'kur. I will use all of my influence as well as commit the forces of my own clanbrothers to defend your lifemate."

"How generous," Ra'kur sneered. "Or it would be if I did not already know the price of this . . . alliance."

"More like me," Jenna said bitterly.

"Mates for my clanbrothers," Mirak agreed. He glanced between Ra'kur and his father. "And yours." He spread his hands. "We will unite and coordinate our efforts. We will limit the importation of human females to a few hundred and forbid any child from being taken from their world."

"Why would I share anything with *you*?" Ra'kur demanded. "If I wanted to use that information for gain, to exploit Jenna's world and gather females from it, why not do it solely for my own enclosure? Why would I ever help yours?"

"As you can see, Mata," Mirak said with a sigh. "The animosity between our clans is longstanding and deep." He narrowed his gaze at Ra'kur. "You must know that every human female you bring home increases the chances another clan will raid your lands, smash your enclosure, steal your females. And the answer to your question, Warrior, is that I have a great deal of influence. I can provide you the support and protection that you need if you wish to bring more here. As well as," he indicated Jenna with a nod of his head, "keep what you already have."

Ra'kur bared his fangs. "Get out!"

"Consider carefully," Mirak warned sharply, "before you reject my offer. There are some on the ruling council who have already suggested the information be taken from you—willing or not. Do you think the others will hesitate to take your mate from you as well?"

Ra'kur stepped forward, his hands curled into fists. "I will not ask you again."

Mirak's own fangs flashed and the guards at the end of the hall tensed. After a moment he took a step back. "Consider what I have said, son of the Erah—and my offer. I hope your clan chooses wisely." He met Jenna's gaze and inclined his head. "Good day, Mata. I look forward to our next meeting."

"That makes one of us," Jenna said coldly.

He gave a half-smile. "And spirited too. I very much regret you are not mate to my son. You may well be worth the trouble of a clan war." He glanced at Ra'kur. "And I am not the only one who thinks you so."

Ke'lar and other Erah clanbrothers formed up behind Mirak and his escort when they stepped into the entrance hall, making it clear that their welcome had just been worn out.

"How could you have let him come here, Father?" Ra'kur demanded.

"What could I have done?" The elder g'hir asked wearily. "He is on the ruling council and stated on his approach he came on official business. The Erah had no reason—or right—to bar him entry to the enclosure."

"Can they really do this?" Jenna asked tightly. "Take me away from here against my will?"

"No!" Ra'kur growled.

Rotin looked away. "Of course not."

Her knees were shaking and Jenna sank down into one of the chairs.

"Jenna?" Ra'kur frowned. "Are you all right?"

She swallowed hard and nodded. In truth though, the whole thing made her sick to her stomach.

"You don't have anything to fear," he said softly. He cupped her face in his warm, broad palm. "I will never let anyone take you away from me."

She gave a faint smile. "I know." She searched his eyes. "It's other women I'm worried about now."

"I will not give Mirak that information," he promised. "I will not make a pact with him."

But she could read in his eyes the truth; a confrontation was coming and there was no avoiding it.

But we have today. We have right now and I'll be damned if I'm going to waste it.

She stood. "Come on, you wanted to show me the orchards, remember?"

Hand in hand they walked into the courtyard and Jenna frowned to see another group of g'hir waiting there. They weren't wearing uniforms like Mirak's guards but the transport and its extended ramp bespoke of their recent arrival.

"More uninvited guests?" Jenna asked quietly. "We just got rid of Mirak."

"Well, I do not know about anyone else"—Si'hala stepped forward from the group of now offended-looking g'hir warriors, and put her well-manicured hand on her hip—"but we *were* invited."

SEVENTEEN

Jenna's face went hot.

Damn it, I keep forgetting how much better they can hear!

"Have we arrived at a bad time?" Si'hala took in Jenna's riding clothes with raised eyebrows.

"We did signal ahead to request entrance to the enclosure," Lihr said, frowning. "But if that permission was relayed in error, we can return another day . . ."

"We mean no offense." Flushing, Ra'kur inclined his head to Si'hala and Lihr. "We bid the Yir clan welcome to the Erah enclosure."

Si'hala exchanged a look with her mate, Lihr, and from the glances the Yir group was sending her way Jenna knew they were waiting for her to do something here. Jenna wasn't sure how to handle this like g'hir would but she could show some human hospitality at least.

"I'm glad you're here too. I'm really happy to see you again, Si'hala." She offered the Yir group a chagrined smile and spread her hands. "Look, I'll be honest, I don't know what a g'hir would do to make you feel welcome but back home I'd suggest y'all come inside so I can fetch you up some sweet iced tea."

"*Ice* tea?" Si'hala raised her eyebrows. "How does one make tea from *ice*?"

"No, it's tea," Jenna assured. "Just cold 'cause it has lots of ice. And sugar."

The visitors stared at her with glowing eyes.

"It is a beverage offered to honored guests," Ra'kur supplied. "As well as one shared by friends. Apparently there is some skill needed in preparing it to the human elders' satisfaction."

Lihr inclined his head. "I would like to sample this cold tea, Mata."

"Oh." She hadn't actually intended to serve them iced tea. "Okay, well . . ." Jenna looked at Ra'kur and gave a shrug. "Point me toward the kitchen and I'll try to figure out how to make some."

Si'hala stepped forward. "I will go with you, Jenna."

"To the *kitchen*?" Lihr wondered, his brow creased as he regarded his mate.

"Oh, why not?" she asked brightly, her many jeweled rings sparkling in the sunlight as she gave an airy wave. "It might be fun. Perhaps I can be of help."

From the look on Lihr's face Jenna could guess that Si'hala's interests didn't usually include much in the way of domestic tasks.

"Ra'kur, why don't you take them into the dining hall?" Jenna suggested with a nod toward the Yir men. "And I'll try to figure out how to make iced tea in time for lun— uh, midmeal."

The kitchen was located not far from the main house's dining hall but it was Jenna's first time inside it. Considering that it sometimes had to serve thousands of guests the space was huge and seemed to be well staffed.

Their arrival there had the cooks—all male, of course—staring wide-eyed.

Jenna caught the attention of the head chef, Tharin. She explained what she needed and he regarded her with the interested eyes of a professional eager to learn any new culinary skills.

The Erah kitchen had a number of different teas on hand. The challenge would be to find one most like black tea and, since the g'hir had a number of different sweeteners—but not sugar—she would have to figure out which one would suit best.

The kitchen staff stole curious glances at them as Jenna oversaw the brewing, icing, and sweetening of the available options. In the end Jenna came up with four different brews and chose two sweeteners she thought would work.

Those two were way too tart, but a third, sweetened with something called cali syrup, was pretty close.

Si'hala was delighted to be included in the sampling but took a sip of the fourth option and grimaced. "Well, it is certainly *sweet*!"

"Back home it gets real hot in summer." Actually Jenna thought this one the closest of the four. "It's gotta be super sweet because the ice melts fast and that makes it just perfect."

Both Tharin and Si'hala, glasses still in hand, regarded her with doubtful looks.

"You know, because it's spring here," Jenna said, "and a heck of a lot cooler, maybe we go with that third one?"

The two gave quick nods of agreement and Tharin gave orders to his staff to start enough tea brewing to serve the new beverage at midmeal. Jenna suddenly wondered how cali syrup would hold up in baking.

"I suppose midmeal will be served soon," Si'hala commented.

"Yeah, I'm getting hungry too." Si'hala was looking at her expectantly and Jenna sighed. "Okay, look, I'm sure I'm supposed to know what to do with a guest, but plain fact is, I don't. What should I be doing right now?"

Si'hala gave her an amused look. "You might offer me a place to refresh my appearance before midmeal."

"Oh, okay." Si'hala already looked perfect, of course, but *she* should certainly change into something more suitable than riding clothes. "Let's go to my quarters and you can fix yourself up there."

Si'hala's bright green eyes took in everything as she followed Jenna upstairs. "It is a fine house. I am sure you will be happy here when you take your place as clanmother."

"Yeah, it's nice." She led Si'hala into her bathroom and to the carved wooden vanity there. The clan, thrilled to have a new female, had provided her with a rainbow of cosmetics, a number of perfumes, and all sorts of hair doodads, way more girl stuff than she'd ever had before. "Help yourself."

"Thank you," Si'hala said, gracefully taking a seat at the vanity. The g'hir woman sought Jenna's gaze in the reflection and her face took on an expression of concern. "I hope your arrival to the enclosure went well? That the Erah clan have made you feel welcome?"

"Absolutely," Jenna said, shifting her weight. "They went all out—feast, streamers, the works."

Si'hala took up an applicator and lightly touched up her already perfect eye makeup. "If you are unhappy here, I am sure you will find there is no end to the suitors you can command."

"I'm happy with Ra'kur," Jenna snapped.

Si'hala's brow creased and she met Jenna's gaze in the reflection again. "It is not my intention to give offense. I just thought if you were unhappy—there are so few females, especially of my own age, and I especially do not wish to lose your friendship. I only meant to help, Jenna."

Seeing the anxiety in Si'hala's face made her think of how her girlfriends had been in Asheville making the most of their twenties while she was moving back to Brittle Bridge to take care of Pap. The responsibility of it put her in a different place in life, creating a gulf that ultimately saw those friendships fade to nothing. It made her different, lonely, and recognizing that same loneliness in Si'hala's eyes now, she softened.

"And I wouldn't want to lose yours. I'm okay here, really." Jenna offered a smile. "Still, it's always nice to hear that you have options, right?"

Si'hala smiled back. "I think you have many, many options."

"You probably had a lot of suitors, huh?" Jenna gave a short laugh. "You must have been the g'hirs' version of Helen of Troy."

Si'hala's eyebrows rose. "Helen of Troy?"

"She was supposed to be the most beautiful woman on my world."

"It is a compliment then?"

"Oh, absolutely," Jenna assured. "Nations went to war over who she would be uh—mated to. She had tons of men after her."

"As must you have had."

Jenna regarded her own reflection, her too-round face, her chocolate brown eyes and hair. "I'm actually considered pretty ordinary for a human."

"But your eyes are so unusual!" Si'hala exclaimed. "Russet with flecks of gold and green throughout. Such smooth, delicate features and your hair alight with a thousand strands of gold and red. Does Ra'kur not tell you how beautiful you are?"

Jenna blinked. "He does but . . . I mean, to me my eyes are just plain brown, my hair is brown too. It has a couple highlights but nothing anyone would notice. I didn't realize I looked any different to him than I do to myself."

"Well, then humans are especially lovely to us then. You look . . . almost supernatural." The g'hir woman's glance went over her and her mouth curved a little. "*Short*, mind you, but still stunning."

"Thanks," Jenna said wryly. "I'm having some trouble getting used to the men staring at me."

"Of course they stare. They see so few females and none like you." Si'hala tilted her head, regarding her with radiant alien eyes. "How do g'hir look to humans?"

Jenna thought about falling backwards onto the snow the first time she saw Ra'kur, screaming as she scrambled to get away.

"A little frightening at first," she admitted. "You're so different from us. The g'hir look beautiful to me now."

"Well, since we are so new to you I do not mind confiding that I would have once been called ordinary looking."

"Uh, I find *that* a little hard to believe."

Si'hala smiled and gave a half shrug. "It is all in how you value yourself, how you carry yourself. Act as if you believe you are beautiful and you *are* beautiful."

"It must be difficult in a way," Jenna said slowly. "To be one of so few women left."

"At no other time in our history would I be so rare, so desired, and mostly I have enjoyed the attention." Si'hala's smile faded. "But my clan pushed me to start considering an alliance when I was only fourteen summers. The wealthiest and most prominent clans sent sons for my consideration. They offered bribes." Her face clouded. "Some made threats against my enclosure if I did not choose one of their clanbrothers. I was well educated, I play a number of musical instruments, but none of that mattered. I could be dull as dirt, a talentless fool, and it would not have mattered. All of my worth lay in my appearance, my value as a fertile mate."

"That's awful," Jenna said.

"And *I* was awful," Si'hala said with a wry smile. "I was scared but I was also haughty, rude, spoiled. When Lihr came to court me I treated him terribly." She gave a laugh. "I was obnoxious—even for me!—and one night he stood up in the middle of our evening meal and told me so. He said he had no wish to spend his life with a miserable brat like me, no matter how pretty I was, and he walked out."

"Wow," Jenna said, her estimation of Lihr going up several notches. "What did you do?"

"Well, I could not believe it! Who was this male to treat me so? But I could not stop thinking about him. To him it was not enough that I should be pretty and female. He wanted more from me, from his mate, he wanted heart and mind and"—she laughed again—"good manners! He among all of them wanted something more of me than my breeding ability, than my looks. Dozens upon dozens of males called to me," Si'hala smiled, "but only Lihr's roar called to my heart."

"What about . . . well, children? They must be pressuring you, all g'hir women, to have as many children as they can."

Si'hala dropped her gaze. "Lihr tries to shield me from the worst of it, but it is always there, following me from room to room like a wraith—When will she have a child? Will she give us daughters or only sons? We have not been mates long and I am young, the doctors assure me I am fertile. The Yir hope I will bear a child to him every year."

"I'm sorry." Jenna put her hand on Si'hala's shoulder. "That's gotta be hard."

Si'hala sighed. "It is the price of being a g'hir female. We are honored, cherished. We have only to stretch our fingers toward something we desire and it is ours, but the survival of our people rests on our shoulders. You are lucky, to be human."

"I don't feel lucky," Jenna said quietly. "Ra'kur and I can't have children, not together anyway. I don't think I even realized how much I wanted them until the doctor told us it wouldn't be possible." She swallowed hard. "He says he doesn't mind, but I know he wishes it were different too."

"He has you," Si'hala said. "His love for you shines in his eyes."

"They want to send other g'hir men to Earth," Jenna blurted. "To my world—to find mates."

The g'hir woman looked sad. "I can understand that. So many are alone and will do—risk—anything to have a lifemate of their own, even a barren one." She turned to look up at Jenna. "There are many who envy Ra'kur," she confided quietly. "I have heard mutters that he should not have you. Some say you should be the mate of a more prominent male. Some say a contest should be held and the winner take you."

"But . . ." Jenna clasped her hands together. "I mean, they can't actually take me away from him, can they?"

Si'hala raised delicate eyebrows. "Not without killing him."

"Wow," Jenna managed. "You really aren't making me feel better here."

The g'hir woman was silent for a moment. "I cannot think of a way to reassure you, Jenna. I do not think any will succeed in taking you from the Erah or from Ra'kur."

"Sometimes I really wish I were just back home on Earth."

Si'hala looked crestfallen. "Is that what you want?"

Jenna dropped her gaze to her hands. "Sometimes. But I can't imagine living without Ra'kur."

"I wish I could advise you better." She gave a wry smile. "I promise when I am not so busy being beautiful, I will endeavor to become wise. But come," she said, standing and shaking off her doleful mood. "We will go and feast and drink icy tea and let them all look at us with admiration and we will be happy." Si'hala gave herself a final check in the mirror and smoothed her honey blond hair. "Your Helen of Troy—she was happy, was she not?"

"Yeah, I think you and I are probably still going to wind up better off than she did," Jenna muttered, turning to her closet to find a dress to change into for midmeal. "Even if her face did launch a thousand ships."

Jenna threw Ra'kur a smile as he joined her on the balcony of their rooms later that evening. "I'll say this for two suns—it certainly makes for an amazing sunset."

"Did you enjoy your visit with Si'hala?" Ra'kur asked, dropping a kiss to her forehead.

"Yeah, she's a hoot," Jenna said fondly, breathing in the cool air of early evening. The Yir clan had left at mid-afternoon with an invitation for her and Ra'kur to visit their enclosure in the coming days. "Lihr is sure eager to show off their hunting lands to you."

"It is the way we forge friendships. To hunt and feast together."

"Their clan hasn't been friends of yours before?"

"We have never been enemies, but have not found any particular reason to ally either." He gently brushed a strand of hair away from her eyes. "We have more in common now that the females who will be clanmothers are friends. I think the alliance will be a strong one."

Three of the kitchen staff came into their quarters then, carrying trays of food.

"What's all this?" Jenna asked as the men set out the dishes on the balcony's table.

"I thought you might prefer to have evening meal here tonight," he said, taking her hand to lead her to the table as the men departed. "I know all the attention is uncomfortable for you."

"That was really thoughtful. And yes," she agreed, sitting. "I'd be grateful for a break."

"What will you have?" he asked. "The braised karlet is Tharin's particular specialty. The cali fruit is freshly picked."

She looked over the spread but shook her head. "You go ahead. I'm not hungry right now."

He gave her a curious glance. "You did not eat much at midmeal today."

She shrugged. She didn't want to hurt his feelings but everything here was so different, so strange, and she was more than a little homesick. The g'hir cuisine wasn't sitting well either.

"I'm just not used to the food here yet. I was thinking that I might head back into the kitchen in the next couple days and experiment with baking here a bit." She gave a grin. "Maybe I could even come up with a passable cheesecake."

His brow creased. "Cheese*cake*?"

She gave a dismissive wave. "Trust me on this one."

There was certainly nothing wrong with *his* appetite and he filled his plate twice.

Jenna was happy with just her hot tea and the quiet. Feeling like she was constantly on-stage was wearing her out and she suddenly wondered if there was anything like coffee on this world.

Another thing that would be worth trying to recreate.

"You know, it's funny." She looked out over the forest, the warm sweet-smelling breeze ruffling her hair, leaning against the balcony railing again at meal's end. She gave him a grin. "Seems like it was winter just a minute ago."

"I did not have the opportunity to show you the orchards today," he reminded and took her hand in his. "They are in full bloom now. We will do so tomorrow if you like. And when you have seen all of our enclosure, we will travel so that you may see more of Hir. The cities and the far-flung settlements of the Pundari Mountains, the wild green oceans of the southern continents. There is so much I wish to share with you."

Her eyes scanned the sky, the unfamiliar stars. "When I was a kid Pap used to point out the different constellations to me and tell me their stories, the myths that went with them. Sure can't see the Big Dipper from here. What was it like, Ra'kur?" she asked suddenly. "The other worlds that you went to?"

He smiled a little, a faraway look in his eyes. "Some were beautiful beyond words, some terrifying. There were months where I wandered from world to world only to find them empty of intelligent life. On some populated worlds I was welcomed, attacked on others. It was an experience that did much to shape who I am now. But of all the wonders I have seen, nothing compares to you." He swallowed. "I love you, Jenna."

She intertwined her fingers with his. "I love you too."

He caught his breath, and then the bright joy in his face faded. "You are sad when you say this."

"It's just—I've been thinking a lot about home." She swallowed hard. "I've been thinking about Pap too, about the land he left me. And about where I belong."

Ra'kur went very still. "You want to return to your own world."

"I'm human. That's where I'm supposed to be—on Earth. That's what I always expected. The life that I was meant to have."

His face worked for a moment. "Please, little bird, give me more time before you decide—"

"I've already decided." Jenna took a deep breath. "And I'm going to stay on Hir."

EIGHTEEN

"You—" His glowing eyes blinked. "You will stay?"

"Yes." Tears stung her eyes and she gave a watery smile. "Not exactly where I grew up thinking I'd wind up—on the other side of the damn galaxy." She traced his jaw. "Spending my life with a man from a species I'd never even heard of. That whole thing with Mirak, just the idea of not being with you . . . It made me realize that those woods that Pap left me—that's not home anymore. Earth isn't home anymore. Home is with you. Home *is* you, Ra'kur. And you were right—we're not going to able to be together there. So we'll live here, on Hir."

He caught her hands between his. His breath released in a sudden rush and she realized he'd been holding it.

"Thank you," he said roughly. "Thank you."

"You don't have to *thank* me," she said with a laugh.

"I was not," he admitted, ducking his head a little. "I was thanking the All Mother."

"I know you've been worried that I'd insist you'd take me back to Earth. That I wouldn't make a life with you. And honestly, if there's any way that I can go back, just for a day or so, to gather some things from the cabin, pictures and recipes, well, that would be great. I'd like to have some reminders of Pap, but he's not there"—she touched the place over her heart—"he's here and he always will be, just like you are. I'm not sure there was ever a question really but, truth is, you giving me the choice made it a whole lot easier to choose you."

He gave a faint smile. "I have feared losing you every moment since that day when you would not let me go for foodstuffs with you."

"Don't remind me," she groaned. "No more root beer floats. Or ice cream. Or pizza. Or chocolate."

He gave her an understanding look. "I liked chocolate."

"Yeah." She sighed. "Me too."

He tilted his head. "This is why you are sad?"

"Hey, as a baker I happen to have a deep—and very meaningful—history with chocolate," Jenna said. "And you, Ra'kur, are the only thing in the whole universe I'd even consider giving it up for."

"Ah. This is an honor then?"

"Huge honor," she agreed, wrapping her arms around his neck. "Tremendous. Really."

"I will endeavor to be worthy of it," he said mock-solemnly, and Jenna gasped as he unexpectedly swung her into his arms. He grinned. "And I will begin right now."

He was already striding toward their bedroom and kicked the door shut behind him. In the next moment he laid her on the softness of the big bed and was sliding his hands up the sides of her thighs, the silky fabric of her skirt bunching up to her hips.

"I have been thinking," he murmured, his eyes hot on her center as he eased her panties down.

"About what?" she asked with a playful smirk as his clothes came off, his cock already at full stand.

Naked now, he knelt between her legs. His fingers ran from her inner thigh to her knee, then he cupped the back of her leg, holding her open.

"About how to show you that you will never, never," he murmured, his rumble purr starting as he leaned forward and pressed his mouth to the inside of her thigh, "wear me out."

He kissed his way up her thigh and then the moist heat of his mouth closed over her clit, the vibration of his rumbling increasing the sensation of his lips and tongue against her a hundred-fold.

Jenna's mouth parted under the onslaught of pleasure, her fingers threading through his hair as his rumbling deepened. She gasped as her climax hit hard but neither his rumble nor his mouth stopped.

The sensation was almost too much. She pushed away a little but just that slight change in position was enough to have her coming again.

Her body felt limp and heavy as he pressed one last feather-light kiss at her center.

"I want to see all of you." He was poised over her, his eyes shining as he undid the fastenings of her dress. "I want to know you are mine."

She shifted to help as he lifted the dress over her head. His gaze ran over her and his eyes softened.

He moved over her, his hard cock at her center, and he shut his eyes halfway, rumbling as he sank into her folds. He nuzzled her neck as he moved inside her, his body arched over hers as he plunged, driving himself deeper as his speed quickened against her.

Jenna wrapped her arms around his neck, breathing in the cinnamon-like scent of him, crying out as he brought her to climax again. His eyes shut and he stiffened, a fine tremble running through him as he came.

Still breathing hard he nuzzled against her, dropping kisses to her cheeks, brushing his nose against hers before shifting to lie beside her.

"You are so soft, so very warm," he murmured, settling against her, skin to skin, wrapping her in his embrace. "My Jenna."

"Actually," she said lightly, reaching to pull the quilt up, "I wouldn't mind a bit more covers." She shivered and pressed closer to him. "Sure doesn't feel like spring now."

"You are so warm." He was silent for a moment. "You always feel cool to me."

With a swiftness that made her gasp Ra'kur caught her wrist, turning her arm to examine her skin.

"What?" Jenna asked, frowning. "What's the matter?"

He didn't answer, staring at her forearm, and she saw it then, faint splotches forming on the inside of her arm.

"Huh." She looked closer at the raised red marks marring her skin. "Kinda looks like the start of poison ivy. I must be allergic to something here. "

"Not hungry. Fever. Blood rash . . ." His head came up, his glowing gaze wild. "The Scourge."

NINETEEN

"I'm not—" She shook her head. "I mean, I've been a little tired but—"

She was frightened, reaching to him for reassurance, and he clasped her slender, delicate hand in his, no longer cool to him at all.

Her fever is rising!

"Ra'kur?"

"The hospital," he said hoarsely.

He quickly tucked the blankets around her. Already he could see the rash spreading, the splotches marring her fine skin, the blood rash that would soon cover her body even as her organs shut down—

"I will go tell them to ready the transport; we must leave for the capital immediately. They will help you there." Ra'kur's heart hammered in his chest as he threw on his clothes. "You are very strong, the doctors said so. They all said so."

Her russet eyes, with their touches of golds and greens, met his. Suddenly he was back in this same house when the Scourge first tore through the enclosure. The halls echoed with the keening of warriors, his father staggering from his mother's deathbed, his face distorted with grief. How he, only eight at the time, held the infant Tarsh wailing in his arms, Ke'lar clinging to him too, their sisters and mother gone forever, three children left trembling as the world crumbled around them—

"There is nothing to fear, little bird." He pressed a kiss to her forehead, his heart squeezing at the heat of her skin against his lips. "They will make you well."

Then he was running, throwing the wooden door to their quarters open so swiftly it damaged the plaster wall, to race down the stairs.

He was maddened, frantic to get out to the transport, so much so that he fought to shake off the man's grasp when another warrior caught him at the foot of the stairs.

"Brother?" It took him a moment to recognize Ke'lar, peering worriedly into his face. "What is it? What has happened?"

"Help me!" he gasped. "Jenna is—ill."

"Ill?" Ke'lar's brow creased. "Is she—?"

Ra'kur shook his head sharply, forcing the words out. "The Scourge."

Ke'lar's eyes widened. "How is that possible?" His gaze went to the stairs, to the level above. "No female has contracted it since—"

"I have been gone *years*!" Ra'kur grabbed his brother's arms like a drowning man. "There must be something now—a treatment—*something* to help her!"

Ke'lar hesitated and Ra'kur's stomach clenched at the unspoken words.

"Ready an escort," Ra'kur rasped, letting him go. "Call ahead to the medical center and tell them—tell them we are coming."

"I will accompany you," Ke'lar offered instantly and then added quietly: "And I will tell Father that Jenna is . . . ill."

Ke'lar took off at a jog. Ra'kur turned and the hall suddenly seemed to swim around him.

There were females who survived the sickness, even at the height of the Scourge. The Goddess will not take her from me now.

Still, he had to clasp the handrail to steady himself enough to get back up the stairs. She was shivering by the time he returned to their room. He quickly wrapped her in the quilt then gathered her into his arms and lifted her from the bed.

"I should get dressed," she protested as he strode for the door, cradling her in his arms.

"There is no need." He focused on using care as he carried her down the steps. "They will only make you change into a smock once we reach the hospital."

"Still, I should have underwear on at least, for heaven's sake." She ventured a smile, a faint splotch forming on the soft curve of her cheek. "Whatever will they think?"

Ke'lar, his father, Tarsh, and a number of the household—warriors, servants, tillers of the land—had gathered in the center hall, their eyes shocked and grieved, silent as he carried her through their midst.

As if they come to mourn her already.

His arms tightened around her and he looked to his brother. In response to his silent question Ke'lar turned to lead the way to the transport that awaited them in the courtyard.

The evening air was growing chill for spring, the transport vessel already powered up. He kept his stride smooth, even as he quickened his pace across the courtyard, anxious to get her on board and inside the warmth of the cabin.

He settled on one of the vessel's upholstered bench seats, she in his lap, disregarding the safety straps so he might keep her in his arms.

She stirred against him, seeking a more comfortable position as the three other clanbrothers accompanying them quietly boarded, their faces grim. They dispensed with the pre-flight check and the transport lifted off the moment the ramp retracted and the outer door was sealed.

As soon as they were in the air, Ke'lar made his way back from the pilot's compartment.

"We will maintain the highest speed possible. I have contacted the medical center." His growl was soft, seeking not to disturb her. "They are summoning the chief physician now. If there is anything else I—any of us—can do . . ."

Ra'kur gave a short nod and with a final look at Jenna, Ke'lar made his way back to the cockpit.

"That's nice," she murmured. "The rocking."

He had not even realized he had been doing it, trying to comfort her, trying to comfort himself.

"We will be there soon," he promised.

"I know how worried you are," she murmured. "You shouldn't be. I'm tough as nails. This virus—or whatever it is—is gonna be sorry it ever messed with a McNally."

"You should rest." He brushed wisps of her hair away from her forehead, her skin hot against his fingers. "Save your strength."

Jenna eyes were a little glazed and splotches of red marred her cheek now. "'Cause we're going dancing later?"

"We are going to the hospital in Be'lyn City," he reminded gently. "You are delirious, beloved."

She gave a quick smile. "No, just got me a lousy sense of timing. I was joking."

"You are ill." He swallowed. "You should not try to cheer me."

"Well, *someone* has to perk things up around here or this road trip's gonna just suck." She wet her lips. "Is there any water?"

"Yes," he mumbled. "Of course."

He signaled to one of his clanbrothers and the man brought him a drinking pouch. He held the straw to her mouth and she drew long swallows but the action seemed to exhaust her.

He resealed the pouch and placed it beside him in case she wanted more.

"I think you're just upset because I'll be seeing Doctor Elaran again. Jealousy," she tsked. "It'll get you into trouble every time."

"He will not lure you away from me." The smile he forced for her sake felt like a grimace. "I will give him no time to flirt with you."

"But promise . . ." she whispered, her eyes closing. "We'll go shopping again. Si'hala . . . snagged all the really good dresses for herself."

"Yes, of course. Anything you wish."

"I'm gonna remind you that you said that." Her eyes opened to meet his gaze. "I love you."

His chest burned with joy and fear. "I love you," he said hoarsely. "My Jenna, my little bird."

A smile flitted across her face and then her eyes closed again. "I think . . . gonna sleep for a little bit . . ."

"Yes," he whispered. "Sleep now."

She settled against him her eyes moving beneath her lids, shadows purpling the skin beneath her eyes. His hand rested on her ribs so he could feel her breathing even as he watched the blood rash spread across her cheek.

He squeezed his eyes shut, willing himself to silence, to swallow back the keening building in his throat.

TWENTY

Sometime later a warm hand touched his shoulder and Ra'kur tore his eyes from her, cradled against his chest, to blink up at his brother.

"We will land in a few moments," Ke'lar murmured. "A medical team is already assembled. They will meet us at the landing platform."

Ra'kur nodded. Her mouth was parted in sleep like a child. Her breathing hadn't become labored yet; that would happen later, when fluid began to fill her lungs.

He stood with her in his arms as soon as the transport touched down and had to force himself forward. She seemed to weigh less to him now, as if her spirit were no longer wholly in her body.

Full darkness had fallen but the landing platform was brightly lit, the wind strong here, so many stories above the ground. A team of four medics, the senior physician and the younger healer, Doctor Selai, were already there with a gurney for her.

"Get her on," Doctor Elaran said to them then threw a stern glance at the medics. "We need to get her straight to Critical and I want one of you monitoring her vitals at all times. First aberrant reading, you report it to me." He nodded at Doctor Selai. "Make absolutely sure the respiration unit has been prepped to accommodate her physiology. I want it ready to go the moment we need it."

The young doctor jogged ahead. The others were standing ready with instruments, waiting for him to turn her over to them.

To let her go.

Ra'kur cradled her close, breathing in her sweet scent, sick with the knowledge that once he released her, he very well might never hold her again.

Gently he laid her on the gurney and took a spare, precious moment to press a kiss to her forehead.

Her eyes fluttered open to look at him, her gaze dull with fever. The rash had reached her other cheek now.

Then they were gone, speeding her away, snapping off readings to each other.

"How long since the symptoms began?" Doctor Elaran asked as they hurried after.

"I do not know," Ra'kur admitted. "She had little appetite today, but I did not think that—a few hours, perhaps more. The rash began tonight. The treatment—"

"I will do everything I can," the senior physician promised as they entered the building.

"My brother said—" Ra'kur glanced back at Ke'lar, who followed them down the hall. "There have been no new infections?"

"We thought the disease had burned itself out but if it is resurging, or if—may the All Mother help us—it has mutated . . . This entire floor has been cleared and we are on quarantine protocols." Doctor Elaran threw a regretful look at him. "That lockdown has to be extended to your entire enclosure."

"The Yir visited us yesterday," Ke'lar reminded. "Council member Mirak as well."

"Damn it," Doctor Elaran muttered. "Until we know more they will have to go under quarantine too and anyone *they* have had contact with."

He waved Doctor Selai over and quickly communicated the information to him. The young physician's eyes were wide and fearful as he went to relay the new instructions to the peacekeepers outside tasked with enforcing infection control.

The medics lifted Jenna onto a hospital bed, crowding around her to insert an IV, to attach skin sensors. Her readings scrolled across screens on every wall, the room filled with medical equipment.

"I think it is best if you wait outside and give us room to work, Warrior," Doctor Elaran said, standing in front of the monitors, making tiny adjustments as he scanned the information. "I will keep you apprised of her condition."

"No," Ra'kur said, not taking his gaze from Jenna. "I will stay with her."

"I truly think—"

"I will not interfere in your efforts," Ra'kur broke in. "I will not hinder you in any way but I will *not* leave her."

Elaran spared him an impatient, frustrated look but seeing that Ra'kur would not be moved, let him be.

The staff circled around her, drawing blood, taking readings. They changed her into a hospital smock, two medics holding a privacy sheet as the doctors examined her. They covered her again, adding several blankets, and raised the temperature of the room to stop her shivering until Ra'kur felt the sweat break out on his forehead.

She was having trouble breathing by then and Jenna batted weakly at the mask as the young doctor fitted it over her face. Ra'kur clenched his fist against the impulse to push them all away. He had to trust them; he had to let them do what they needed to do to heal her.

One of the medics came to his side, silently offering him something. Ra'kur put out his hand and the man gently put Jenna's little gold bird necklace into his palm.

He blinked down at it, gleaming faintly in his hand under the light of the medical monitors. It was a lovely, delicate thing, its tiny wings spread as if poised to fly away any moment, still warm from resting against her skin . . .

Doctor Elaran touched his arm. "Come outside, please. We need to speak."

Jenna's eyes were closed, most of her face obscured by the breathing mask. Swallowing hard, Ra'kur slipped her necklace securely into his pocket then followed the doctor into the hall.

"You have a decision to make," Doctor Elaran began as soon as the door shut behind them.

"Whatever will help her," Ra'kur said hoarsely. "Whatever she needs."

"To extend her life she will be on total support and with the amount of pain medication she'll need she won't be conscious but—"

Ra'kur felt the floor tilt away from him as the doctor's meaning came clear. "There must be something you can do! A treatment you can try, anything—"

"We can address the symptoms," the doctor interrupted. "But the disease itself has no cure. I had hoped . . . but the blood rash has already spread to over eighty-five percent of her body. In my experience, when the Scourge has reached this stage the patient has a few hours at most."

Ra'kur shook his head. "No . . ."

"I am truly sorry." Doctor Elaran said. "I can make her comfortable—"

"*No!*" Ra'kur roared and in an instant had the doctor by the throat. "You must save her! You must treat her!"

"This is the Scourge!" Doctor Elaran gasped, struggling. "There *is* no treatment!"

"Let him go, Ra'kur!" Ke'lar cried, trying to peel his hands off the physician. "Let him go! This will not help her!"

No, nothing will.

He released the man and the doctor fell back, gasping.

Ra'kur caught himself against the wall, recalling the ragged sound of his own breath from his run, Jenna dying in his arms from the peacekeeper's weapon. Remembered watching desperately for the stasis indicator light to know that he had made it to the ship in time, how his fingers, stained with her blood shook as he raced through the final recalibration, praying the whole time to the All Mother . . .

But he had hope then.

He felt so numb now he could not even form a prayer.

"I brought her to Hir," he murmured, his hand pressed hard to the wall to keep himself upright. "This is my fault."

"You could not know—" Ke'lar began.

"She did not want to come! She did not want to leave her world at all." Ra'kur swallowed hard. "I should have gone then, before I was discovered. Left her in peace, but I loved her, so very much. . . I could not bear to be parted from her. I cannot now." He met Ke'lar eyes. "I have killed her, Brother."

"It has been so long since any female has become ill . . ." Ke'lar shook his head. "None of us could have known."

"My Jenna." Ra'kur closed his eyes. "I have killed her . . ."

"Brother," Ke'lar urged, his hand on Ra'kur's shoulder. "Be with her now, while you can."

He was right; there would be time enough for grieving.

I will have the rest of my life for that.

Ra'kur sought the doctor's gaze. "You said . . . Promise you will not let her feel pain."

"She will not," the doctor said quietly. "I give you my word."

Ra'kur swallowed hard and made his way to her bedside. She was asleep, resting easy now despite the breathing mask over her face, the rash that covered her now. She looked so delicate lying there, so fragile.

One of the medics carried in a chair for him and he could not even summon the words to thank the man as he set it at her bedside. The medics and doctors withdrew to a respectful distance. There was nothing they could do now, save keep her comfortable.

There was nothing he could do but be with her.

Ra'kur sank down and took her slender hand between his, marveling again at the softness of her skin, the softness of her being.

He was dimly aware of the others as the hours passed, how one of the doctors would draw near to check one thing or another and then retreat again.

Ra'kur watched her with stinging eyes, his life condensed to the spaces between one of her breaths and the next.

Sometime near morning Jenna stirred, her eyelids fluttering, and his grip tightened, desperate to hold her here, to keep her with him.

She turned her face toward him and her brow creased when she met his gaze. She pulled at the mask weakly with her other hand, her voice muffled by it. "Stupid . . . thing off . . ."

The young doctor hurried over. Selai exchanged a glance with him then removed the breathing mask.

Once free of it she turned her face toward him. "Ra'kur . . ."

He leaned close. "I am here, little bird. I have been here the whole time. I will never leave you." He brushed her hair away from her eyes. "Do you hurt? The doctors have medicines they can give you for the pain."

She waved her other hand dismissively and after a moment, Doctor Selai stepped back.

"Do you want something?" Ra'kur pressed a kiss to her hand, and held her palm against his cheek. "Whatever it is you want, you will have it."

She wet her lips. "Pancakes."

He blinked. "What?"

"I want pancakes," she repeated. "With bacon. And muffins."

His brow furrowed.

"Oh, come on," she urged when he did not answer. "You guys gotta have *something* like pancakes, right?"

"Are you saying you are . . ." He shook his head a little. "You are hungry?"

"Ra'kur—" Jenna shifted toward him, her beautiful eyes clear and focused on him. "I am freaking *starving*."

Every occupant of the room went still. In the next moment Doctor Elaran was across the room, standing at her bedside, checking her readings, his fingers flying over the displays.

"How is this possible?" Elaran shook his head, his brilliant yellow eyes wide. "The virus is dying. By the All Mother," he croaked, "she has beaten the Scourge."

TWENTY-ONE

"Jenna . . ." Ra'kur warned.

"Well, I'm sorry but this . . . *fucking* . . . *itches*!" Jenna snapped, scowling up at him three days later from her hospital bed, clenching her fists to stop from scratching.

She might have recovered but the illness had left behind a rash that was making her miserable. It wasn't the blood rash, the Scourge was undetectable in her system, but whatever it was her doctors had no clue how to treat it.

"You'd think a society that has figured out how to travel across space using wormholes would have something comparable to goddamn Benadryl!" she grumbled.

He examined the array of creams and lotions that Doctor Elaran had left for them to try. The ward was still in lockdown and Doctor Elaran refused to even consider lifting it till she was completely symptom free for forty-eight hours. And that clock didn't even *start* till she could lose the damn rash.

"You must not scratch," he said. Again.

"It's driving me crazy!"

She shouldn't be scratching—or bitching—she *knew* that. G'hir females had died by the millions from the Scourge and even those who survived scarcely clung to life for weeks before inching their way to recovery. The only good part of that was children born to those women had a natural immunity to the illness.

But apparently Zerar biological weapons were no match for a *human* immune system. In fact, Hir's top immunologists were already hard at work to replicate the antibodies from her blood to develop a vaccine so the Scourge would never be an issue again.

To the astonishment of her doctors she'd been up and about in less than twenty-four hours. She still felt intermittently queasy but her appetite had returned with a vengeance and for the first time ever she could out-eat Ra'kur.

For the most part she felt great.

Except for the stupid, annoying, sadistic-ants-tickling-her-skin-with-a-feather *itch*.

"Jenna!" Ra'kur scolded as he turned back and caught her about to dig her nails into her forearm again.

"Fine!" she gritted out. "I'll sit on my damned hands!"

"I know you are uncomfortable," he said, rubbing yet another cream into the skin of her forearm.

"And you must be going nuts with boredom. I know Ke'lar and the others can't wait to get out of here."

"You are well," he said, washing the cream from his hands at the sink. "I have need for nothing else. And my clanbrothers are warriors. Warriors must have patience."

"They're certainly getting some good practice here."

"You must not worry for them," he said firmly. "You must concentrate on your own health."

"Actually I'd like to think about something else. And most of all I'd like to get out of here."

"I can understand that," Doctor Elaran agreed as he joined them.

"Sorry," she said, embarrassed to be caught complaining.

The hospital staff too was on lockdown in the ward until she was symptom-free. Meals and supplies were sent in and since the ward had been cleared there were plenty of rooms, beds, and space for those stuck inside. But with all of one patient whose only complaint was dermatitis, the four medics and two doctors didn't have much to occupy them either.

"Do not be," Doctor Elaran said with a smile. "I am only thankful the Scourge has not returned to Hir, and your resistance so remarkable to it. We have been fortunate indeed." He nodded at her arm where Ra'kur had applied the newest cream. "Any improvement?"

"No," Jenna admitted, miserable. "I only wish there were."

Doctor Elaran pursed his lips for a moment. "Let me take a look and see if there is any change to the skin on your back from the ointments we applied earlier. Midmeal has just been delivered but I would like to do a quick exam first."

"Why don't you go grab something to eat?" she said to Ra'kur. With so much time on their hands meals were a welcome distraction for everyone. "I'll be right out."

He pressed a kiss to her forehead. "I will see if they have sent the icy tea you like this time."

"It's really called 'iced tea' where I come from," she said to Doctor Elaran as soon as Ra'kur closed the door behind him. "But I kinda like that he calls it 'icy tea.'"

He gave a smile and, moving her gown aside, peered at the skin of her shoulder, his fingers gentle as he probed. "And none of the creams have given you any relief?"

"No," she said, holding up her forearm where Ra'kur had applied the new one to show him. "The itching is just the same with all of them."

"I wanted to run through all of the topical options first. I have something else that I know will work," the doctor said, readjusting her hospital gown to cover her shoulder again. He held up a metal cylinder. "But it is an injection."

Jenna gritted her teeth, using all her willpower not to dig her nails into her skin. "Frankly, right now I wouldn't care if you had to administer it with a cannon. How long will it take to work?"

Doctor Elaran placed the injector against her skin. "Immediately."

The injection stung a bit.

"Are you sure that's going to work?" Jenna asked, frowning against the impulse to scratch as he placed the cylinder on the table beside her. "I mean I still kinda . . . Hold on, I think—something's—"

Elaran raised his eyes to meet hers.

He had a funny look on his face.

She gasped, trying to draw breath, and her hand went to her closing throat. "Can't—"

"I am truly sorry." Doctor Elaran rested his hands on her shoulders, holding her in place, his face heavy with regret. "It will be over quickly."

Holy fuck, he's killing me!

For an instant she was back in that college dorm room, Ricky screaming in her face as he threw her against the wall, his hands at her throat, trying to crush the life out of her. He'd been a football player, big as a Mack truck, and she'd fought because she knew if she didn't she'd die.

Just like now.

She snapped out a kick and caught the doctor square in the balls with her heel. Moaning, he went down and she managed to draw a thin tiny breath, like sucking wind through a bitty little straw.

She made a grab at the table and lurched for the door. She had a few seconds at most before he recovered enough to grab hold of her again.

It was three spare steps across the room, each more of an effort than the last. She stumbled, catching herself against the door.

Her vision was going black at the edges as she slid downwards. With a final effort she slapped the door control and fell face forward into the hall, the syringe of whatever he'd injected into her still gripped in her hand.

TWENTY-TWO

"Jenna?" The growled words in her ear were soft, urgent. "Little bird, can you hear me?"

Jenna forced her eyes open. Ra'kur hovered over her, holding her hand between his. His face registered relief when she met his gaze.

Her glance flickered around the room, the familiar feel of a mattress beneath her. The young blond healer—Doctor Selai—was frowning and splitting his attention between her and the readings scrolling over her hospital bed.

Doctor Elaran was there too, held between two of Ra'kur's clanbrothers. She drew her breath in and flinched when she saw him.

"He—tried to—!"

"You are safe now," Ra'kur soothed. "He will never hurt you again."

"Can I have some water?" Her throat felt scratchy and sore. "Please?"

Doctor Selai took a water pouch from the side table and held the straw to her mouth himself.

After a few swallows, her throat didn't feel as raw. She gave Selai a nod of thanks and gestured to Ra'kur to help her sit up in the bed.

"How am I?" she asked Selai, craning her neck to see the scrolling alien readout—not that it made any more sense to her now.

"Lucky," he said. "And smart. I wouldn't have known how to reverse the effects if you did not have the syringe in your hand to tell me what to counteract. We got to you in time to prevent any permanent damage." He jerked his chin at her. "How do you feel?"

"Shaky. A little woozy." She glanced at Doctor Elaran. Despite the fact that he'd just tried to murder her, he looked burdened, grieved, and not evil at all. "On the bright side whatever he tried to kill me with got rid of the itching."

"No," Doctor Selai said tightly. "*That* cure was simple. It seems he has been purposefully withholding the proper treatment." Selai threw a disgusted look at his disgraced colleague. "In order to keep you here until he could find an opportunity to murder you."

"Why?" Jenna asked sharply. "Why would you want to kill me?"

"To save my world!" Elaran cried. "And yours!"

"He is insane!" Ra'kur snarled.

"What are you talking about? Save my—" Jenna shook her head. "You mean because I got the Scourge?"

"No," the doctor growled. "Because you are pregnant."

Ra'kur's head snapped around. "What?"

"*What?*" Jenna cried. "What the hell are you talking about?"

Doctor Selai adjusted the monitor and his mouth parted as the readings changed. "I did not even scan for—I did not even think—!"

"But I *can't* be!" Jenna insisted. "I haven't been with anyone except Ra'kur for—seriously!—*years*. The only way I could be pregnant is—"

Her gaze met Ra'kur's.

"The child is mine?" he asked hoarsely.

"By the All Mother . . ." Doctor Selai murmured, blinking up at the screen then at Jenna. "Half-human." He looked at Ra'kur. "Half-g'hir."

"You lied," Jenna whispered, staring at Elaran, and then her voice rose. "You told us we could never have a child. You said it was impossible!"

Doctor Elaran's face was taut. "I made the discovery when you were first brought to the hospital. The tests meant to help replicate blood for your injury uncovered something I did not expect. To be sure I did a full comparison of your genetic makeup and ours." He sent a pleading look at Doctor Selai. "Look for yourself. Human DNA is part of the g'hir genome!"

"You are saying we are a hybrid species?" Doctor Selai asked, frowning. "How is that—"

"I do not know!" Doctor Elaran closed his eyes briefly. "The only explanation is that far back in our history, interbreeding with humans—or *a* human—must have occurred. Our phenotypes are obviously quite different, but—as you can see for yourself—procreation with humans is possible."

"We—" Ra'kur's throat worked. "We are going to have a child?"

"I had the Scourge. I was so sick. Is—" She was afraid to ask. She had never been so afraid of anything in her life. "Is the baby okay?"

Doctor Selai looked at the screen. "Well, I cannot claim expertise in the field of half-human half-g'hir babies," he muttered. "But everything I am seeing here indicates you should bear a healthy female child."

"A baby. A baby girl. I can't believe it," Jenna murmured, caught between grinning and tears. "Ra'kur, we're going to have a baby!"

In the next moment she was in his arms. She could feel his trembling joy as he held her.

"I had hoped to end her life before anyone else could discover the truth." Doctor Elaran threw a wild glance around at them. "*Now* do you—all of you—understand?"

"No," Jenna said sharply. "No, I—for one—fucking well *don't*!"

"Nor do I," Doctor Selai said, turning to face him.

"Your actions are those of a madman." Ra'kur's eyes narrowed. "Do you not understand, fool? This is the saving of our people! We will not die out, this child signifies hope for all g'hir!"

"There will be no more g'hir!" Elaran spat. "There will only be half-breeds!"

"Every child—*any* child—is a gift to our kind now!" Ra'kur snapped. "Who are *you* to condemn our males to live out their lives alone? To decide our people should die out?"

"Hold on," Jenna said. "You said you discovered it when you were first treating me. That's why I didn't come out of stasis like I should have? Because you tried to make sure I wouldn't?"

"You should not have been able to," Doctor Elaran admitted. "I do not know how you did."

"I do," Jenna murmured, remembering Ra'kur keening at her bedside. Then her head came up. "All those tests you did the last time I was in the hospital . . . *That's* why I got sick when no one else has in so long. You son of a bitch! *You* infected me with the Scourge!"

Elaran closed his eyes briefly. "I knew if you died of the same illness that the Zerar used to kill so many of our women—if our people believed human females were just as vulnerable to the Scourge—no others would seek your kind out as mates, they would not bring more of you here. Why do so, just to watch you all die?"

"You are a monster!" Ra'kur roared, his arms tightening around Jenna. "To inflict the Scourge upon her! You are worse than the Zerar!"

"Your actions are more than criminal, they are evil." Doctor Selai shook his head. "You were my teacher, my mentor . . ."

Ra'kur went still. "I brought you here," he whispered and his face blanched. "*I* gave you over to this beast, I trusted him to care for you. I failed you—"

"No, Warrior." Selai's shoulders slumped. "It was I who did not question his diagnosis. I did not examine the test results with the diligence I should have. This is my fault."

"Oh, no, hell no!" she warned them with a sharp glance. "This is no one's fault but *his*!" Her nostrils flared as she turned her glare on Elaran. "Nothing but a low-down lying, murderous—!"

"I was a young physician here, in this very hospital, when the Scourge came. I watched while our females died by the *millions*!" Elaran's hands curled into fists. "I will not stand by and let the Zerar defeat us now! To intermate with your kind—it will give them their victory, for we will no longer be truly g'hir!" His yellow eyes were stormy and he shook his head. "I sought only to preserve my kind, to keep our enemies from destroying us. I would never have wished you harm. I have nothing against you personally."

"Well, that there is where I'm done gonna have to disagree with you, Sawbones." Jenna's eyes narrowed. "In my opinion, trying to kill me makes it pretty fucking personal!"

"What do you think the Zerar will do to your world, Jenna?" Elaran demanded. "When they discover there is a hope our people will survive? And what do you think the *g'hir* will do to your world?"

Ra'kur bared his fangs. "Get him out of here," he snarled to the clanbrothers holding the doctor between them. "We will take him before the ruling council. We *will* have justice for these crimes!"

Jenna closed her eyes as the door shut behind them and Doctor Selai. "Oh my God . . ."

"Jenna?" Ra'kur asked quickly. "What is it?"

"He's right," Jenna said. "He's right about how your people are going to react when they find out. The men here already want what you have. What do you think they'll do now that they'll know human women can give them children too?"

Ra'kur searched her eyes. "Why is that so terrible—to want a mate, a child?"

"But they'll raid Earth, conquer it if they have to! They'll go and they'll *take* women from there—whether they want to go or not."

"We will not do that," Ra'kur said tightly. "My people are not monsters, we are not all like Elaran."

"Your people are hunters." She swallowed hard. "And they're desperate. They won't want to wait or show caution. They won't care about how it will affect my people or my world, just that they'll save their own. And what about the Zerar? If your enemies would use the Scourge against you, why wouldn't they try to destroy my world too?" Tears stung her eyes. "What are we going to do?"

"I am the only one who knows how to reach your world, Jenna. We will safeguard Earth as best we can." He enfolded her hand with his and his gaze softened. "But for now, little bird, you are well. We are together and we are going to have a daughter of our own. Let our minds rest joyfully on that for now. A daughter with eyes like yours."

She took a deep breath and let it out. "Yeah, you're right. We have to make the most of what we have right now." She smiled and intertwined her fingers with his. "Hey, I bet when she cuts her teeth she'll have cute little baby fangs."

TWENTY-THREE

"I think that's enough pillows," Jenna said gently as Ra'kur tucked yet another one between her side and the wooden bench, the orchard of the Erah enclosure warm and fragrant around them.

Zels—the slow-moving bumblebee-like insects of this world—flitted from flower to flower, filling the sunny afternoon with the sound of their humming as Jenna settled back. She tilted her head up to feel the warmth of Hir's suns on her face, breathing in the sweet fragrance of the cali trees' purple and white blooms.

There was no keeping this kind of thing quiet and news of her pregnancy had already spread across Hir, but if she thought the clan doted on her before, it was nothing compared to now. She'd beaten the Scourge, she was carrying the first child the Erah clan had in years; she was the hope of an entire race.

She wasn't even showing and the entire clan was distressed if she even frowned.

That's probably why he brought her out here today.

"You are worried."

She fingered the bird charm around her neck as Ra'kur sat next to her. "Of course I am. The ruling council is going to start sending warriors to Earth any day now. I hate that we had to help them at all."

"I know. But as soon as they seized my ship they began to extrapolate the location of your world. They were going to find it even without my help; it was only a matter of time," he said, taking her hand in his. "Recall the concessions we were able to force from them in return."

She nodded dispiritedly. The agreement they'd made with the ruling council gave the warriors who brought women back twenty-nine days to convince them to stay. If the women didn't agree, if they wanted to go home, they had to be returned to Earth.

It just didn't feel like they'd done *enough*.

"But now there's the Purists to deal with," she pointed out. Doctor Elaran wasn't alone in his conviction in preventing the g'hir from producing "half-breeds." Most males were eager to be chosen, a very few so much so that they argued for full-scale invasion of Earth while a small but vocal group calling themselves "Purists" were vehemently opposed to any intermating with humans at all. Certainly Yalar, mother of the two girls, wasn't happy about a half-human baby stealing some of her children's thunder at the enclosure—or the possibility of more human females coming to Hir. "And we're still talking about women being forcibly taken from their homes."

He brushed her hair away from her eyes gently. "Are you not happy—here—with me, my Jenna?"

"Of course I am. I love you. You know that. And you know I'm gonna give any Purist a right good piece of my mind, but we aren't talking about me."

"These women will be given everything they could wish for. They will be honored, cherished—"

"They'll be kidnapped, terrified, miserable—"

"As you are?" he countered, hurt.

"No, of course I'm not. But I *chose* this."

"Not at first," he reminded. "You did not wish to leave your homeworld. You would not have come here at all."

"At least I knew you! They're talking about hunting women down like animals!"

"To capture a mate is the g'hir way."

"The g'hir way," she said. "Not the human way."

"The competition to go to your world is fierce. These warriors know how fortunate they are to be chosen. Only one will be permitted to go this time and only a handful have even been deemed worthy to be allowed to in the coming months." He searched her eyes. "Would you deny it to them? Those who have suffered years upon years of hopeless loneliness? Who want only another to share their life with? Who long to have a family of their own, as we will have?"

He was right. Doctor Elaran was spending his life at a penal colony for trying to keep this chance from his people and he was lucky to get off so easily in the face of public outrage. These men—these people—had every right to try to survive.

But not at someone else's expense.

Ra'kur looked toward the distant orchard gate and then stood, waving in greeting to the g'hir warrior there.

"Who's that?" Jenna asked, standing too as the unfamiliar man started their way.

"I thought you would like to meet the first warrior the ruling council has chosen to voyage to Earth," Ra'kur said with a nod at him as the man joined them. "This is R'har."

He was tall, of course, and powerfully built as any of their warriors. His hair was a pale golden blond; his glowing green eyes were good-humored.

And really familiar.

Jenna tilted her head. "I've seen you before, haven't I?"

"Yes, Mata." R'har inclined his head. "I am of the Yir clan."

"Sure, I remember you now. You were one of the clanbrothers who escorted Si'hala last time she visited."

"Yes." R'har's eyes positively sparkled with anticipation. "And I am deeply honored to be chosen to seek my own mate among your kind."

"Yeah," Jenna murmured. Maybe she was wrong to worry about this, maybe the human woman that got R'har would consider herself lucky as hell. The ruling council had certainly chosen the first warrior well: he was intelligent, mannerly, and some kinda gorgeous.

"The council has given me only a single moon cycle to convince a female to be become my lifemate. I know I must choose a remote area, that I must remain clandestine in my search. I have studied all the information they gave me but I have come to beg for your wisdom." He tilted his head. "Have you any further guidance for me, Mata? To call a human female to me?"

Jenna shifted her weight. "Uh, you know, I don't know how much they emphasized this but you really want to hold off on the mating roar. You'll probably just frighten her."

R'har blinked and a rush of concern filled his green eyes. "*Frighten* her?"

"Look, whoever she is, I can promise she won't have seen an alien before. She won't know what you are. Think of human females as delicate, fragile things." Jenna laid her hand on his arm. "Things that don't really like getting roared at."

He looked genuinely worried now. "How do I call her to me then? My chosen one?"

"Just be gentle and kind to her." Jenna gave an impish grin. "Oh, and don't hold back on the mating-rumble thing. That's definitely a winner."

"But how can I make her love me?" he asked. "I have only a short time to convince her to be mate-bound to me."

"Well, that I can't tell you, R'har, even if you were human yourself." She patted his arm. "It's okay. You'll figure it out."

She met Ra'kur's radiant blue gaze resting lovingly on her and she smiled. "And remember, just because she's not expecting you, doesn't mean you aren't exactly what she's been looking for all along."

WARRIORS OF HIR SERIES
BOOK TWO

Willow Danes

TAKEN

WARRIORS OF HIR

TAKEN

Hope MacGowan is a city girl but reeling from a
break-up on top of a layoff has her determined to have
a weekend away in the North Carolina mountains—
even if all her friends have bailed at the last minute.
Hope's life is one big train-wreck and getting
kidnapped by a tall, blond alien—even a gorgeous
one—sure isn't helping.

R'har crossed the galaxy to seek a mate on this newly
discovered world and this delicate red-haired female is
everything he's dreamed of—except happy to find
herself mated to him. R'har knows in his heart he's her

true mate, even if he's not human. But taking her doesn't mean he can keep her and somehow he has to convince Hope to choose him before time runs out . . .

Available Winter 2014

ACKNOWLEDGMENTS

Many thanks to my editor, Erin McCabe. Working with her is always a joy!

Thanks to my cover designer Steven James Catizone for your talent and, especially, your patience.

Thank you to everyone who supported and encouraged me and, most of all, to my family.

Willow Danes

Willow Danes is the pen name of author Ariel MacArran. She loves all genres of Romance but especially Sci-fi, Paranormal and Historical.

Novels written as Willow Danes:

Science Fiction (Warriors of Hir Series)
> *Captured*
> *Taken*
> *Stolen*

Novels written as Ariel MacArran:

Historical
> *Another Man's Bride*

Science Fiction (Tellaran Series)
> *The Seer*
> *Stardancer*
> *The Consort*